WE DON'T NEED NO

STINKING BADGES

The Hollywood Murder Mysteries

PETER S. FISCHER

THE GROVE POINT PRESS
Pacific Grove, California

Also by Peter S. Fischer
THE BLOOD OF TYRANTS
THE TERROR OF TYRANTS

The Hollywood Murder Mysteries
JEZEBEL IN BLUE SATIN

FOR GEOFF
who got it all started.

CHAPTER ONE

Bogie's at it again and I can't believe it.

Sure, three or four years ago he was a bundle of TNT waiting for someone to light his fuse. He was tossed out of Ciro's and El Morocco and The Stork Club and a dozen other adult watering holes that catered to the rich and pampered. Some, but not all, even made his banishment permanent. When he was juiced enough he was ready to take a poke at Rocky Graziano with his wife Mayo egging him on, she just as juiced as he was. But then along came Lauren Bacall and in a matter of months America's favorite bad boy grew up years. It was said that his self-loathing just fell away like a stripper's spangles and he began to regard Johnnie Walker, not as a bosom buddy, but as an acquaintance to be handled with care.

It is very early in the morning. I am sitting in the middle of the living room of my newly acquired house in Van Nuys, surrounded by a motley assortment of furniture and unopened boxes and staring at my phone which I have just hung up. Although I was given the day off to finish moving in, I have now been told to get my butt over to the studio in Burbank chop-chop and don't make any plans for the next week or so and oh, yes, bring your passport. I know what this means. I am on my way to Mexico.

According to Charlie Berger, the head of press relations and my immediate boss, Bogart is sitting in a Tampico hoosegow after tearing up a local cantina around midnight the previous evening. Charlie doesn't know the exact charge or the amount of damages but I've been elected to deal with it. He gives me the name of Carlos Martinez who is the Director of the Mexican National Film Commission. Carlos will assist in every way he can. It has been my experience that this means he will be almost no help at all but maybe in this instance I am wrong. These things happen when you are the new boy in town and I have been employed by Warner Brothers for exactly twenty-seven days. It doesn't get any newer than that.

I look around at the stacked chairs, covered sofa, rickety tables and chipped lamps, all relics of earlier days in my Western Avenue apartment. I had been afraid none of it would fit but this house is so tiny that I think I will have nothing to worry about. The boxes contain my books, my record collection, cookware and dishes and other incidentals. My clothes are still packed in two suitcases sitting on the floor of my bedroom. My bed is leaning up against the wall in pieces. Not to worry, I will not be sleeping here for several days. In the meantime, elves may come in and take care of things for me. They are known to do that, at least according to the fairy tales I've read.

I pick up the phone and dial The Hollywood Reporter where I ask for Bunny Lesher. Bunny is a dynamite gal who has it all and luckily, she wants to share it all with me. She's a writer and reporter and she knows her job but between the sheets she and I manage to keep her priorities and mine separated. Most of the time. There are exceptions.

"This is Bunny Lesher," she says.

"I can tell from the dulcet tones," I say.

"Oh, are you listening with your good ear?" she replies.

"Intently."

"You'd better not be calling to break our date tonight," she warns.

"Alas----" I start to say.

"Joe, this is the second time this week. Who the hell have you got on the side and don't tell me Lydia or I'm hanging up." Lydia is my ex-wife and a sore subject for us both.

"Tell you what," I say. "Dinner's still on if you like Mexican food and you can talk Wilkerson into giving you a round trip ticket to Tampico." Billy Wilkerson, editor and publisher of The Reporter, is her boss.

"Ah, Bogart!" she says brightly.

"What do you mean, Ah Bogart?" I say.

"And did you think I was deaf , dumb and blind with no clue as to what is happening in the world around me? He's in the slammer and I now see that you've been saddled with the task of calming roiling waters."

"Astutely stated."

"And how long do you expect to be calming the roiling?" she asks.

"They say a week, but who knows?" I reply.

"I'll miss you," she says.

"As well you should," I say.

"Although there is this new guy in ad sales----- "

"An ad salesman? If you're that desperate, go for it."

"On the other hand I could demonstrate loyalty and patience until your return----"

"An excellent idea."

"---especially if you were to call me late tonight with a first hand account of the situation so that I might write it up and impress my boss and thereby perhaps earn myself a raise or at the very least, a bonus."

"And how might your journalistic competitors feel about that sort of favoritism?" I ask.

"Like crap," she says.

"In that case, I'll consider it."

We chat like that for a few more minutes and I continue to realize what a great broad she is. We have a terrific relationship. Fun times, good sex, and mutual trust and respect. If I were ever to think about marrying again she'd be the one but at the moment, I'm in mid-air between the euphoria of the ether and the harsh reality of solid ground. I like where I am. I think I will stay there for a while longer.

Later that day I am sitting in a window seat of an American Airlines Condor 990 heading for Brownsville, Texas, where I will change to a Mexicana flight to Tampico. I am not flying first class. Warner Brothers, notorious penny pinchers in every phase of filmmaking, are even cheaper when it comes to press and publicity. Jack Warner apparently resents every dime he spends on every press release and our department has the budget to prove it. My pay is appallingly meager but since it was the only offer I got since my return to Los Angeles three months ago, my stomach and I voted to accept it. My per diem will cover my expenses providing I don't eat breakfast or lunch. I would rather be spending my time working on my novel which is about sixty per cent complete and I tell myself that all of this is only a temporary way station on my way to the Pulitzer Prize. My capacity for self-delusion is boundless. I devote one or two hours to it maybe twice a week if I'm lucky. At this rate, by the time I finish the book, chances are no one will remember who Pulitzer was.

I put aside these grumblings of self-pity and try to sleep but the engine is noisy and uneven and rather than being lulling and soothing, it's just annoying. I am probably being an ingrate. At my last job, Continental Studios, transportation was confined to car, truck, bus or very occasionally, the train. Warner Brothers has slightly more class and unlike Continental, is not fighting it out with Monogram for the title of crummiest studio in Hollywood.

In my lap is the script for "The Treasure of the Sierra Madre" which is the film that is shooting on location in Tampico. In fact the film is supposed to be shot entirely within Mexico with exteriors set for the district of Durango on the other side of the country. I remember reading the book by B. Traven while I was stationed in Germany following VE day and I recall that it was pretty grim stuff. Well written but depressing and I wonder why they are filming it. Are they hoping for a big box office success? I just can't see it. The studio gossip mill says the picture is in trouble. Jack Warner has hated the project from Day One. He has seen the rushes shipped overnight by courier and he now hates it even more. It is over budget and threatening to spin out of control. If this were any other picture it would have been shut down a week ago but the driving force behind this project is writer-director John Huston who has enough muscle to do whatever he wants and if he is able to buffalo Jack Warner, then more power to him. In any case, familiarity with the screenplay can only help if I start getting into extended conversations with the cast and crew.

I almost fall asleep twice while reading the script but by the time I get to 'Fade Out', I pretty much know the story. Bogie is playing a down and out none too honest grifter named Fred C. Dobbs who hooks up with a young kid named Curtin played by Tim Holt and an old prospector named Howard played by Walter Huston who claims to know where gold can be found in the Sierra Madre mountains. Walter is John Huston's father and while he is in the twilight of his career, he is a genuine Hollywood icon, revered and liked by almost everyone. Barton MacLane's also in the cast playing a crooked contractor who tries to cheat Bogie and Tim Holt out of their wages. They beat him up to get their money and then use it as a stake to equip themselves for prospecting. The three of them eventually find the gold and that is where the distrust and greed start to take over. It is the over-riding theme of the film. A stranger tries to force his way into their group, sensing they have hit it rich and Bogie and the oth-ers are on the verge of murdering him when the bandits inter-rupt. The bandits threaten to rob and kill them and in the end, Bogie's character is murdered and his gold dust confiscated. But the bandits, thinking it is merely sand, open the bags and send all of it wafting into the wind. As I said, pretty much a downer.

I must have dozed off because suddenly I am hearing the squeal of tires and the jolt of wheels hitting the runway and I look out the window to see the control tower of the Brownsville airport. It is a few minutes past two and the sun is still bright overhead and I don't need a thermometer to tell me that outside it is hotter than Hell's front door. When I alight, I am not proved wrong.

I duck into the main building to grab a burger and a cold drink. The lunch presentation on the flight from L.A. would win no blue ribbons from Betty Crocker and my stomach is making noises like a tomcat in heat. I have less than an hour to layover before I board the Mexicana DC3 for Tampico. I start to scan the available material at the tiny newsstand off in the corner. I pass over the dime western pulp magazines and snatch up the last remaining copy of The Reader's Digest. I am intrigued by one of the titles within: 'How to Double Your Income With Half the Effort'. I know it's nonsense but I'm intrigued enough to find out how they are going to validate the title. As I am standing there a man in an American Airlines uniform approaches me.

"Mr. Bernardi?"

I nod. "I'm Joe Bernardi."

"There is a telegram for you, sir, at the reservation desk," he says.

I thank him and walk cautiously to the desk, wondering, as Dorothy Parker once observed, what fresh hell can this be? I say this with the certain knowledge that Western Union seldom, if ever, is the bearer of good tidings. The cute little clerk whose name tag reads "Conchita" smiles and hands me the wire. I smile back and rip open the envelope. It's from Charlie and reads as follows: "Forgot to mention. Huston has invited book author B. Traven to visit the set. If he shows, be helpful but handle with kid gloves. Man is reclusive, almost a hermit. May actually be wanted by authorities for anti-government activities. If things get out of hand, use your best judgement. C. Berger."

I have to laugh although the situation is far from funny. Our star is in jail. It's possible the press may suddenly show up to turn his incarceration into an international incident and to top it off, I may have a creepy bomb-throwing writer to contend with. And if things turn to horse puckey, who will assume the burden of guilt for any unfortunate incidents? Why the fellow who has been with the studio for only twenty-seven days. Charlie Berger, you are a sly self-protective dog.

Forty minutes later I hear the first call for my Mexicana flight and I head for the exit. As I step out into the sunlight a cab pulls up and a familiar figure steps out of the back seat. Harry Frakes is the movie columnist for the Los Angeles Herald-Examiner and not a person you would wish to spend a lot of time with, unless, of course, you are a fan of vacuous opinions on every subject under the sun.

I avert my face, hoping he didn't see me but it's too late.

"Joe!" he calls out heartily.

"Harry," I respond less heartily.

"Looks like we're going to the same place," he says.

"Looks like," I say obviously.

"Great," he says. "It'll give us a chance to get better acquainted. Maybe give me the inside dope on all that business last year at Continental."

That is a subject I have no intention of discussing with Harry or anybody else but my job forces me to be polite so I smile politely.

We board the plane and as I settle into my seat, Harry settles in next to me. I can see this is going to be a very long flight. He tells me he flew into Brownsville yesterday to do an interview with Ken Maynard who was grand marshal of the city's annual rodeo. He got a call from the paper about the business with Bogie and was told to check it out.

"Way I see it, best way to check something out is face to face, right, Joe?" he says.

"Right," I say restricting my responses to one syllable.

"So what's the story with Bogart?" he asks. "Fell off the wagon or what?"

"Don't know yet. When I know, you'll know," I tell him.

"Nice of you, Joe, but I'll just do a little digging on my own."

He then proceeds to tell me all about Tampico, the best restaurants, the classiest bars and some not so classy, the red light district, the back room casinos, and the guy you go to see to beat the currency exchange. I am nodding all the while, eyelids drooping, when it suddenly occurs to me I might be able to put this compendium of trivial information to good use.

"I suppose you've read the book, Harry," I venture.

He snorts. "Several times, most recently last night . Pretty depressing material. No wonder Bogart got drunk. This shows every sign of being a real stinkeroo."

"What about this guy who wrote it? I hear all kinds of things," I say.

"Traven? A real piece of work. Most of what you've heard is probably true." He then launches into a blow by blow of Traven's checkered life. Born in Chicago, raised in Germany, anti-social to the core. Opposed to whoever was in power and acted upon it. Street riots, sabotage, bombings, pamphleteering, intimidation, he was up to his neck in all of it. Fled Germany one step ahead of the law, ended up in a London prison and finally emigrated to Mexico. He started writing about the downtrodden native population, the abject poverty and the lack of opportunity. He was suspected of, and questioned about, dozens of anti-government attacks in the Chiapas region where revolution was beginning to foment within the Mayan population. No charges were ever brought but it was no secret that the government was terrified of his notoriety and influence. Throughout this period Traven made few if any close friends and kept to himself to the point of disappearing for months at a time.

By the time we get to Tampico I know more about Bruno Traven than I know about myself. I learn one other thing as well. Harry Frakes has a photographic memory and remembers anything he has ever read. This explains why he is such an incredible bore. Had it not been for the pilot's announcement that we were about to land, he would still be talking and I would be fast asleep.

I alight from the plane leaving Frakes behind to wrestle with his carry-on bags and to look for his glasses which he seems to have misplaced. There's a beat up Jeep sitting there and the young man behind the wheel leaps from the car and waves to me. He's a good looking Hispanic and it suddenly occurs to me that I am going to have severe communications problem with the locals as my Spanish is basically limited to "si, si", "buenos dias" and "gracias".

I needn't have worried. As he approaches, he says to me in perfect English, "Hi, Mr. Bernardi. Welcome to Tampico. Jimbo Ochoa at your service." His grin is infectious. I learn that his given name is Jaime, that he was born and raised in Los Angeles, and that he got the job of second assistant director because he spoke impeccable English and Spanish, unlike most of the American crew.

Jimbo hustles off to collect my bag and I take a moment to scan my surroundings. It is hot but at seven p.m. not oppressively so and the sky is a clear beautiful blue, the way it used to look in L.A. before the automobile started to choke the streets with its fumes. Jimbo returns and tosses my suitcase in the back of the jeep just as Harry Frakes is deplaning.

"Let's get out of here, Jimbo," I say.

He follows my look toward the plane. "So we're losing the guy in the cheap suit?"

"You catch on quick," I say.

"That's me, boss. Sharp as a blue blade."

I glower at him. "Vamoose, amigo!"

He grabs the wheel and guns the engine and grins as we speed toward the airport exit.

"Gee, Mr. Bernardi, I thought you told me you didn't speak Spanish," he says and then winks.

I wink back which is when I notice the scabs healing on the knuckles of both hands. I've seen enough bar fights to know what that means. Bright and breezy Jimbo is apparently no one to fool with.

CHAPTER TWO

Jimbo skitters the jeep to a stop at the front entrance of the Paloma Blanca, the hotel that is serving as location headquarters for the company. The ride from the airport was an adventure with Jimbo avoiding about 40% of the potholes and discovering about 60% of the ruts. I call that a draw. My kidneys call it inhuman.

The hotel looks inviting enough. Whitewashed exterior, Spanish tile roof, three stories of rooms, some with balconies. A huge veranda fronts the hotel and many of the guests are lounging on wicker chairs and enjoying beverages of various blends and brews. I'm not sure if this is pre-dinner or post. I'm not up on the dining customs in Mexico though I am aware that in Spain, the evening meal is often not taken until at least ten p.m. This my stomach will be unable to deal with.

Jimbo is carrying my bag and we are headed for the front steps when a police car pulls up. Bogart gets out of the passenger side, then leans in and exchanges a few pleasantries with the driver. As the cop car pulls away, Bogie starts for the entrance. He's wearing a white cotton suit with an open collared shirt and for a man who was supposed to have terrorized a cantina the night before and spent a dozen hours in jail, he looks both happy and healthy.

"Mr. Bogart!" I call out, hoping to catch him before he goes in. He turns and I hurry to him, introducing myself.

He sticks out his hand and smiles that crooked smile of his. "Nice to meet you, Joe," he says, "You plan to be with us long?"

I hold the door open for him as he goes in, me right behind him. "Not if I can help it," I say.

"Good man," he says. "Haven't met a hotel room yet that can match your own bedroom."

I smile. "I don't suppose you've got about five minutes. I have to call the studio and let them know what's going on and who better to tell me than the man himself?" I smile even wider.

"Sure, Joe. Let's go in the bar."

He leads the way. He's not a tall man or a big man but people move aside when he approaches. Often they smile shyly. He smiles back, even giving them an occasional "Hi" or "Howyadoin'?" This is not the surly loner Bogart that I've heard so much about. I look back and see Jimbo at the registration desk with my bag. He's signing me in and gives me a thumbs up.

As we start into the bar a young kid passes us coming out. He looks Mexican but I don't think he is. I say to Bogie, "I think I know that kid."

Bogie looks. "Bobby Blake," he says.

"Who?"

"Kid actor. Used to be in the Our Gang comedies. Last couple of years he's been playing Little Beaver in the Red Ryder series," Bogie tells me.

"What's he doing here?"

"He plays the kid who sells me a winning lottery ticket. Bobby's kind of snot-nosed little bastard but he can act."

Bogie finds a quiet table near the back of the room and when the waitress takes our order, he opts for a Mexican beer. I have the same. He grabs a handful of salted peanuts from the bowl on the table and starts popping them into his mouth.

"They kept you there a pretty long time, it looks like." I say.

He shakes his head. "No, I was out first thing this morning. I was playing chess last night with the Chief but we never finished so I went over this afternoon to give him a lesson. You know what that lesson was, Joe? Never play chess with a movie actor who sits around a set most of the day with nothing better to do than improve his chess game." He grins and just then our waitress delivers our beers. He raises his glass. "Prosit."

"What happened to 'Here's looking at you, kid'?" I ask.

He laughs. "Another time, another place. Besides you're no Bergman." I salute him with a sip of my own. "So how's the screenplay coming along?"

"What screenplay?" I ask.

Bogie grins. "Don't kid me, Joe. All of you guys have a screenplay in the drawer. It comes with the job."

"Not me," I laugh. "Mine's a novel."

Bogie arches an eyebrow. "Excuse me, we have an author in the house."

"Not yet. I still have a ways to go."

"Well, keep at it. If you're still doing this stuff twenty years from now, you'll probably want to blow your brains out."

We both laugh and throw down some more beer.

"So I guess they dropped the charges," I say.

"There were no charges," Bogie says. "All a big misunderstanding. There were only five of us in the place at the time. Around midnight. I was having a beer with Jack Holt. You remember Jack Holt?"

"Sure," I say. "Jeanette McDonald dumped him for Gable in 'San Francisco'."

"That's the guy. Anyway, he's down here with a one-line part, just a throwaway as a favor to his kid."

"Tim," I say.

He nods. "Right. So we're both nursing beers---that's mostly what I drink these days--- when all of a sudden these two guys across fhe way start beating up on the third fella. Well, hell, it's none of my business so Jack and I keep sipping and talking when suddenly somebody tosses a chair in my direction so I pick it up and I throw it back and just about then is when the policia drops in. We all got a ride to the station including Jack who said he'd never been in a jail in his life."

"How'd he take it?"

Bogie grinned. "He loved it. Something to tell his grandchildren."

I frown. "So let me get this straight. You don't get locked up, you start playing chess with the police chief."

"You catch on quick. Jack hightails it to the hotel and the other three bozos get locked up. Last I looked they were still there."

I smile. "You know this is going to make a terrific story."

"Gotta be better than the one they're spreading around now."

"Bogie!"

I hear a man's voice behind me and turn as a man in a tan linen suit hurries to the table. He's 30'ish, skeleton-like with pale skin and slicked back brown hair. He's wearing a pinkish shirt with a baby blue tie and on his feet are highly polished saddle shoes. I doubt that he is one of the locals.

"Whatdayasay, Phil," Bogie says without enthusiasm, rubbing his index finger under his bottom lip.

"Good to see you, Bogie. We pulled a few strings to get you out of there. Guess you knew that," Phil says.

"No, actually I didn't, Phil, since neither Jack Holt nor I were ever charged."

He looks confused. "Oh, but I thought---"

Bogie overrides him. "Phil, this is Joe Bernardi, he's with the press department. Joe, Phil Drago, associate producer."

Drago gives me a sharp look which Bogie doesn't see because he is draining his glass. He gets up. "I need a shower and an hour's worth of shut eye. I'll see you boys later. Nice meeting you, Joe." He salutes me and goes off.

"I'll check with you later, Bogie," Drago says, calling after him. Bogie either doesn't hear or doesn't care. Drago turns his attention to me.

"You just arrived, Bernardi, so I'll let this one slide but from now on, remember one thing. Mr. Bogart is off limits."

"What? Are you kidding me?"

"Do I sound like I'm kidding?" Drago says.

"And just why is Mr. Bogart off limits to the studio publicity department?" I ask.

"His free time is valuable. If your need to see him is urgent enough I'll make the arrangements."

"If you don't mind, I think I'll run that by Mr. Blanke," I say. Henry Blanke is the producer of the movie.

"Mr. Blanke is back at the studio. He won't join the company until the move to Durango. Until then I'm in charge and your job is dealing with the members of the press and cranking out news stories, not chatting with our cast."

I furrow my brow in concern. "Have you heard that Mr. Blanke is suddenly deceased?"

"Of course not," Drago snorts.

"Good," I say. "Then he'll be taking my call and I can put an end to this bullshit."

"Be careful, Mr. Bernardi. Don't question my authority."

"Mr. Drago, I am starting to question everything about you so listen carefully. I am going to do my job as I see fit and if the studio wishes to fire me or yank me back to Los Angeles, so be it. But in the meantime, stay out of my way."

I start to go, then point to the bill that the waitress has left on our table. "Take care of that, will you, Phil? Thanks."

I head for the desk to pick up my room key. In the lobby I spot Harry Frakes buttonholing Tim Holt who looks as if he'd rather be back in Monument Valley shooting another nickel-and-dime western. I've heard Tim is a nice young man. I make a mental note to hook up with him early in the morning and try not to talk him to death.

My room is neat and clean and small and has no balcony. Jimbo has already told me to keep my windows wide open at night after the sun goes down to catch the cool breezes coming in off the Gulf of Mexico. My bag is on my bed and it doesn't take me long to unpack.

I put a call in to the Mexican Film Commission honcho, Carlos Martinez, who is staying at a different hotel. He does not answer the phone in his room and I leave a message to have him call me.

I take out a pad of lined paper and spend twenty minutes at a small work desk composing a story based on Bogie's account of his so-called arrest. I reach for the phone and ask the long distance operator to connect me with the studio. I know Henry Blanke will have gone home by now but I get the press office and I dictate to one of the stenos on duty a press release for first thing tomorrow morning. Then I have the operator put me through to Bunny.

"Hi, it's me," I say.

"How's the weather?"

"Oppressively hot and soakingly humid," I respond.

"Miss me yet?" she asks.

"You're constantly in my thoughts."

"I can't believe you ever get anywhere with a line like that?"

"It works beautifully on feeble minded women who fail to understand the devious twists and turns of the male libido."

"That's the little boy talking," she says.

"Actually, the little boy is doing nothing right now and he is very lonesome," I say.

"Okay," she says."Enough of this raucous sex talk. What about Bogart?"

I read to her exactly what I read to the studio steno.

"I gave it a nine a.m. release so anything you can do earlier, you've got the beat," I say.

"Great," she says. "The presses don't lock until midnight . I can get it in tomorrow's edition. What about Harry Frakes? I hear he's there along with Phineas Ogilvy from the Times."

"Frakes busted my eardrums on the way down. Phineas I haven't seen but I'll give it to them both first thing in the morning, ahead of the release time so they'll think they owe me one."

"Good move," she says.

We bill and coo for a few minutes more and then I hang up because I am being assaulted by hunger pangs. I check my watch which says 7:56 but it may be two hours later Tampico time and I think I'd better head for the restaurant before it closes for the night. Visions of a steak and baked potato dance in my head.

I am straightening my tie in the mirror when there is a knock on the door. "It's open," I call out. The door opens and a man in a Panama hat peers into the room. He is short, overweight and sweaty with a roundish face and sideburns down to his jawline.

He is wearing a jacket and a tie but his shirt is not buttoned and his tie is pulled down and his jacket could use a good pressing.

"Senor Bernardi?" he asks hopefully.

"That's me," I say.

He beams, "Muy bueno. I am Carlos Martinez from the film commission. I was downstairs talking to Senor Drago and before I left I called my hotel for messages. I am so happy to make your acquaintance."

He barrels toward me with hand extended, daring me to shake. I do. His hand is hot and clammy. Rivulets of sweat pour down his neck from his jowls and disappear down his shirt front. The man seems genetically unsuited for this climate.

He asks about my flight. I tell him it was fine. Have I had any problems? None I know of, I say, but I've only been here a couple of hours. He laughs nervously.

"I wish you to know that I am at your service, Senor. Any difficulty whatsoever. The police, the merchants, immigration. It is my job to see that you are treated like a visiting dignitary."

"I'll try to remember that," I tell him.

"Bueno. And if on the remote chance you do encounter some small problem, I would take it as a courtesy if you would bring it to me first."

"If you wish."

"Muchas gracias. And now I see you are getting ready to dine so I will trouble you no further. Again, Senor, bienvenudo a Mexico." He tips his Panama hat and leaves. My immediate impression is that this man is not a bulwark of fortitude so why is he so anxious to have first crack at any stumbling blocks I may run into? I see a contradiction here. I also see that whatever problems I run into will almost certainly be mine alone to solve.

I needn't have worried about the kitchen. It is in full swing and so is the restaurant. A mariachi band is playing for the entertainment of the guests, mainly crew, and there isn't a seat to be had. I spot Jimbo Ochoa at a table for four with two others, huddled in serious conversation. I wave to him, pointing to his empty chair. He waves me over to join them.

I sit down, order a beer and scan the menu. No steak, no baked potato but a lot of things I've never heard of whose names end in a vowel. Jimbo sees my distress and vouches for the chicken quesadilla. He introduces me to his buddies. Ken Moody is the camera operator and Moe Levine is the lens puller.

I smile. "So what's the gloomy news?" I ask. "You three look like you'd heard Adolf was still alive and restarting the war."

The three of them share a look.

Jimbo says, "Off the record? We don't want this spread around the western hemisphere. We've already been warned twice to keep our mouths shut."

I raise my hand and give the Boy Scout pledge of honor.

"Sabotage," Jimbo says.

This is news to me. "What kind of sabotage?"

"You name it," Ken says. "Three days ago I check my lenses and find three of them cracked. They're kept in velvet lined boxes so it can't happen unless it was deliberate. I had to send back to the studio for replacements. Cost us at least a half a day."

Moe nods. "Night before last someone opened up some water valves and flooded a street we were going to use the next morning. The mud was ankle deep. Maybe another half a day lost while we found another place to shoot."

"Do you know who's behind it?" I ask.

I look around the table. The three of them are looking at each other.

"Go ahead, Jimbo. Tell him," Ken says.

"Maybe we just ought to drop it," Jimbo says.

"I'll tell you what happened," Ken says. "Two nights ago Jimbo goes to the transportation area and catches these two bastards pouring sugar into the gas tank of the catering truck. He yells at them and instead of running, these morons decide to duke it out."

"Ken---" Jimbo starts to say, shaking his head but Ken ignores him.

"Not a smooth move because these guys are unaware that our guy here is a former army Ranger. He beats the crap out of both of them and sends them running for their Mamas---"

"Okay, that's enough," Jimbo says, embarrassed.

"So who were these guys?" I ask.

"We have a pretty good idea," Moe chimes in.

"When we first got here," Jimbo says, "we hired about thirty locals to help out, dig trenches, lay track, do some construction. The local jefe-- that means gangster--- thinks we should have hired ninety. You figure it out."

I shake my head. "This is the first I've heard of it."

"Thank DumDum Drago for that," Jimbo says. "I went to him, told him what happened, he says forget about it. I said we ought to call the police. No, he says, like he's going to take my head off. Why? Because he's scared shitless Blanke or Warner wlll find out and fire his ass so we keep our mouths shut. But he can't keep it quiet forever, not if we have to keep phoning back to the studio for more and more replacement equipment."

I nod. "Makes sense. Well, I gave my word so I'll keep quiet but if more stuff like this happens, you let me know."

Jimbo says he will and I dig into my chicken quesadilla which turns out to be really good but all the while I'm beginning to wonder what kind of a rat's nest I have gotten myself into.

A while later I am heading off to bed. I stop at the desk and leave notes for Harry Frakes and Phineas Ogilvy telling them to meet me for breakfast at eight o'clock if they want a scoop on the rest of the world. As I head for the staircase, I spot Phil Drago in animated conversation with the director, John Huston. I can't hear the words but I can see Drago sweating and Huston looking like a man who'd like to start a brawl. Maybe tomorrow I can find out what that is all about but right now all I can think of is getting some sleep.

My room is warm, even with the windows wide open. I strip down to my skivvies and lay on top of the sheets. Tired as I am, dozing off shouldn't be a problem but I toss and turn. I can't turn off my brain. The alarm clock on the dresser sounds like a jackhammer---tick, tick, tick---and I consider tossing it out the window. I think I may have gone into a light stupor because when I hear the car horn blaring, I look up at the clock and it reads 1:44. The horn gets louder and I hear some shouting so I get up and go to my window and look down into the courtyard that fronts the hotel. A shiny Cadillac limousine comes to a halt and the driver leaps out and scurries around to the open the rear door as people begin to gather. A nicely put together woman gets out. She's got red hair and is dressed all in white with a white floppy hat. I can't quite see her face but then she looks up and I think she might actually be looking directly at me. I can't believe my eyes.

Ann Sheridan?

What in God's name is Ann Sheridan doing here?

CHAPTER THREE

At eight o'clock the hotel restaurant is pretty much deserted which is when I remember that the crew call was for 6:30. On location, filming starts early and quits late. Hotel rooms and per diems are expensive so you cram into ten days what would normally take twelve back at the studio.

Phineas Ogilvy is sitting alone at a table in the middle of the room, drinking coffee and eating something which he later tells me are huevos rancheros. To his left is a basket of bread and a jar of jam. To his right is a platter of sausages and some kind of brown beans.

He smiles as I sit down. "I started without you, old top," he says. "Hunger brings out the rudeness in me." I smile and tell him it's quite all right. I am to learn that for Phineas, hunger is a permanent condition. He is a big man, over six feet tall and big all over, most noticeably around his waistline. He wears his hair long and carefully tousled and I think, though I am not sure, that he uses just a hint of blush and a trace of eyeshadow. He is not homosexual and has three ex-wives and five children to prove it but he is by any measure a flamboyant character who doesn't care what people think of him as long as they think of him. He is also mensa-level smart and possessed of a wit that would do Oscar Wilde proud. The Los Angeles Times is lucky to have him.

"How did you sleep last night?" I ask.

He gives me a sly grin. "Why, on my back with my arms folded across my chest. How did you sleep, Joseph?"

I shake my head with a smile. "Guess I walked into that one."

"Sometimes, Joe, you're not even a challenge." He shakes his head.

The waitress approaches. I take a second look at Phineas' feast and opt for less. Toast and jam, juice and coffee.

"So, Joseph, tell me. What is the glamorous Madame Sheridan doing at this god-forsaken location?" he asks.

"I don't know about now but last night it was the tango with Tim Holt." I reply, dead-pan.

He frowns, then smiles and shakes a finger at me. I shake back. Touche.

"Well, Phineas, to tell you the truth, I don't know but as soon as I find out, you will be among the first to know."

He gulps some coffee and starts to sop up some egg yolk with a half-eaten piece of toast. "I love it, Joe, when you fellows start off with 'to tell the truth' causing me and my fellows scriveners to wonder what you might be telling us without that comforting reassurance."

"Okay, I'll rephrase. I haven't a clue but I will find out."

"And after you tell the beauteous Miss Lesher, you will tell me." He smiles. I smile back.

Just then Harry Frakes arrives, winded, but I am sure not too winded to start talking so I beat him to the punch.

"Ah, there you are, Harry. Just in time. I've only got a minute so sit down and listen carefully. Got your notepad? Good, because I can only go through this once." His mouth is open as if he'd like to say something but I don't give him the chance. I give him the Bogie anecdote and they both take copious notes. Phineas is grinning. I hope I get a chance to read his take on this misadventure. I'm sure it will be wryly mischievious.

A few minutes later I am walking along one of the main thoroughfares, heading toward the location.The jeep was parked outside the front entrance but I didn't see Jimbo so I decided to hoof it. No problem. I have precise directions. By now I've gotten familiar with the location set up. The production office takes up two large rooms at the back of the first floor. Next door to the hotel is an office building and we have rented out the basement to serve as a darkroom for film developing and a place where the film editor can start splicing scenes together under Huston's direction. This dank place is affectionately known as 'The Cave'. The rushes from previous days shooting are screened at noon at the Alameda, a nearby movie theater which is open to the public starting at 5:00 p.m. Burt Yarrow, the unit production manager, has given me a list of all the locations and maps to help me find them so I am pretty well oriented.

I cross a plaza and head down a side street, then stop and turn as I hear a man call out my name.

He's dressed in dungarees and a light cotton short sleeved shirt which he wears outside of his trousers. He looks to be in his mid 40's with a thin scraggy build. His face is not familiar nor is his name when he gives it to me.

"Pedro Castano," he says putting out his hand. We shake. "I do not think you know me, Senor Bernardi. I have a small but significant part in this film but my scenes wlll not be shot until we get to Durango."

I take a wild stab. "Gold Hat?" I surmise.

He grins from ear to ear.

"At your service," he says. "You are walking to the set? So am I. We wlll walk together. I am making it my business to get to know everyone. This is good business for an actor, would you not agree?"

I tell him I do. Castano will be playing the crazy but vicous head bandido. It's a flashy part. Small but memorable. It comes to me suddenly that I know this man's name.

"The Man from Vera Cruz," I say to him.

He smiles. "Si. El Hombre Vera Cruzano."

"I didn't see it but I remember reading about it. You got excellent notices."

He shrugs. "I have received many flattering reviews but the Mexican film industry, it is not so important . We labor in anonymity and the pay is small. I have a wife and two children and also awards and honors but these awards and honors do not pay the bills. To make this American movie, this is a privilege and also a great opportunity. I would like to make more. Perhaps like my good friend Ricardo Montalban."

"I've met Ricardo. A nice man."

"And some day he will be a big star in America," Castano says. "I wonder, Mr. Bernardi, if perhaps you could write a small story about me, not just for the Mexican periodicos but for your American audience as well."

"I can do that," I tell him.

"Gracias, senor. My Luisa will be so proud. We have been married twenty years next month and she has been waiting a long time for me to be truly recognized. A wonderful woman. Very patient. Very understanding. Are you married, Senor Bernardi?"

"Not any more," I say.

"I am truly sorry. I was married young. Perhaps for you it

will happen later. To find the right woman, to have children as I do, you will be many times blessed."

Thoughts of my ex-wife Lydia cross my mind and I want nothing to do with them. I change the subject. "So, Pedro, have you met Phineas Ogilvy yet? The writer for the Los Angeles Times?"

"I have not had the privilege," Castano replies.

"I'll introduce you," I say. "You'll like him and I think he'll like you."

"Gracias, senor," Castano says.

"De nada," I say, dredging up more of my limited vocabulary. "What do you think about all the trouble we've been having," I say.

"What trouble is that, senor?" he asks blankly.

"The water flooding the street, the broken camera lenses," I say.

He shrugs dismissively. "This is the movie business. These things happen." He looks at me, then looks away quickly. He knows all about the sabotage but he doesn't want to talk about it. What's he hiding and why?

"No, Pedro," I say, "these things don't happen." I look him in the eye.

"No, they don't," he says. "Not in your country but this is Mexico, Senor Bernardi. A land of great potential which has never been realized. Enterprising men make their own opportunities."

"You can't be condoning what's going on."

"Certainly not but people like El Jefe, they cannot be brought down. They are too self protective."

"But the law---"

"The law can do nothing!" he says sharply. He is immediately contrite. "I am sorry. My outburst was unforgiveable. But I know how it is in your country. You make jokes about the Mexican police. The corruption, the incompetence. No, no, I do not mean you personally, Senor, but it is a known fact that Mexican law is not held in high esteem among your people. But I tell you this. I have many friends who serve with the police. Many years ago I myself was an officer of the law."

I'm surprised by that. "Really? Tell me about it."

"There is nothing to tell. That part of my life is behind me. I mention it only so you might give my thoughts credence." He hesitates. I think in the heat of the moment he feels he has said too much. To change the subject, he points ahead to a cross street about ten blocks away which looks to be crowded with people. "That is where we are filming today. Many people come to watch. This is much excitement for them, especially to see Mr. Bogart. He is very popular among my people."

Just then I hear the beep-beep of a horn and Jimbo and his jeep pull to a stop next to us.

"Anybody need a lift?" he asks, smiling.

I gauge the distance and decide I've had enough exercise for the day. "Muchas gracias," I say hopping in.

"Senor Castano?" Jimbo asks.

Castano regards him stiffly. "I am perfectly capable of walking," he says stiffly and continues on down the sidewalk.

Jimbo shrugs and we drive off.

"What was that all about?" I ask.

"Castano's got a hard-on for me," Jimbo says. "He brought a medical report from his own doctor. You know everybody needs to be checked. It's part of the contract. I told him his paper was no good, that he had to be seen by our doctor and he got really shitty about it. Hey, I don't care. No physical, no work."

I glance back a couple of blocks at Castano walking. "You think he has something wrong with him?"

Jimbo shrugs. "Not my problem."

At the next cross street, he suddenly turns left and pulls over to the curb. "Look, Joe--- Mr. Bernardi," he says, "I --uh--- I kind of have a situation and maybe you could help me with it."

"Sure," I say instinctively but I can tell from his tone, this is nothing minor.

"I talked to Katey last night. That's my wife. She's eight months pregnant----"

"Congratulations!" I barge in.

"Yeah, thanks. It's our first." He wrings his hands nervously. "Last night she went to the hospital. It was a false alarm but she's scared stiff and she's pretty sure today or tomorrow'll be the real thing. Hell, if I'd known this was going to happen I never would have taken this job. I'd like to go home for a few days, to be there, but when I asked Mr. Drago, he turned me down."

"Son of a bitch," I mutter to myself.

"Katey likes to think she's tough, Joe, but she's not. All she's got is me and an aunt and a kid brother and without me there---." He stops, shaking his head. "If I go over Mr. Drago's head and call the studio, it might cost me my job and for sure he'll never hire me again. So I'm stuck unless--and this is a really big favor—if you could talk to him. I just want a couple of days. Three at the most."

His eyes are pleading and it's been hard for him to ask and I want to help. But I know better. Phil's a tight assed martinet who thrives on power. He'll turn me down flat and laugh doing it. But still I want to give Jimbo some hope.

"It's a long shot, Jimbo. I doubt he'll listen to me but I'll try," I say.

The smile returns. "Thanks, Joe. You're a good guy, you really are."

Feeling a lot better, he does a u-ey and and then speeds down the main street toward the crowd. The director, John Huston, has just turned the set over to the cinematographer, Ted McCord, for lighting. Huston's wearing wardrobe for his role as an American tourist and I suspect this is one of the scenes where Bogie tries to hit up Huston for a handout. Huston occasionally acts and he's not bad at it. I decide this is as good a time as any to pay my respects to our director.

"Mr. Huston?" I say.

He has plopped into his folding chair and he turns to look at me. "Yes?" he says with his rich voice about six decibels below basso.

I tell him my name and he brightens.

"Ah, yes, the press representative. Bogie tells me you're a pretty nice fellow."

"So is Bogie, contrary to the scurrilous rumors that have dogged him throughout his career. Mind if I sit for a minute?"

"Help yourself," he says.

I pull up a nearby folding chair with 'CAST' stenciled on the back. There is no cast around except for Huston and Bogie and Bogie has his own chair.

"I see we've been joined by Miss Sheridan," I say.

"Yes," he says without enthusiasm, looking away and watching the lights and reflectors being put in place.

"I had no idea she was connected to this project," I say.

"Neither did I," Huston says "but I doubt she'll be with us long." Huston can see that I am puzzled. "She was the brainstorm of our associate producer, Mr. Drago, who got it into his head that this dark and disturbing film about three of life's losers suddenly needed a female love interest."

I'm astounded. "For Bogie?"

"Certainly not for my father," Huston laughs.

"Then that little spat I observed in the lobby last night----" I let it hang.

"Very observant, Mr. Bernardi."

"Joe. Please. Just Joe."

"All right, Joe. Mr. Drago suffers from a variety of delusions, one of which is that he is producing this film and another is that he has the talent to do so. I find the best way to handle him is to ignore him or laugh at him, depending on the circumstances. If I were you I would do the same."

"Good advice, Mr. Huston. I'll remember it."

"That's John," he says.

"John," I nod.

Just then another company jeep pulls up and a man hurries to Huston's side.

"Mr. Huston, two men just arrived at the hotel. They say they drove all the way from Mexico City and they insist on seeing you."

Huston wrinkles his brow. "Is one of them named Traven?"

"They wouldn't give their names, sir. They said they were here at your invitation."

Huston looks at me with a smile. "The author doth arriveth," he says. Then to the messenger. "Tell them to check in, get comfortable and I'll meet them in the bar as soon as I get this scene in the can."

"Yes, sir." The messenger turns and hurries off.

"The reclusive Mr. Traven is honoring us with his presence. I am delighted, Joe. Delighted." He hesitates thoughtflly. "Say, why don't you join us," he says.

"If I wouldn't be in the way---"

"Nonsense. From what I hear Traven is quite a character and I think you might get a lot of favorable press out of him if you handle him right. You know people have been trying to interview him for over twenty years, ever since the book came out. He's a pretty elusive character."

"So I've heard. Thanks for the invitation."

He smiles, then just as quickly scowls as he looks toward the set-up. He hoists himself from his chair and strides quickly toward the cameraman. "Ted! No, that's not right. Tell that guy he's too close to the dolly track."

It's just past noon and Huston and I are sitting at a table in the hotel bar which is pretty much deserted. The crew is getting a catered lunch out on the set. Huston has ordered a shot of tequila with a beer on the side. I tried to order a mineral water but when he frowned at me, I switched to beer. Apparently Huston doesn't like to drink alone.

One of the company's security guards is parked by the entrance to make sure we are not disturbed and when a man in a grey gabardine suit appears and looks around, the guard gets up to intercept him. They exchange words and then the guard looks to Huston who waves the stranger in. He is a small thin man with a long nose and close cropped thinning hair and as he approaches, Huston rises to greet him, extending his hand.

"Mr. Traven," he says, "I am delighted to meet you at last."

"You are most kind, Mr Huston, but I am not Bruno Traven. My name is Hal Croves, one of Bruno's closest friends. I believe this will explain my presence here." He takes an envelope from his pocket and hands it to Huston.

Huston sits as he opens the envelope, gesturing to an empty chair. "Please sit, Mr. Croves," He reads the letter. The waitress approaches. Croves orders a beer.

"As you can see, Bruno has been detained by the press of business and asked me to come in his stead. I am authorized to speak in his name and whatever help or information you might have required of him, you need only ask me and I will do my best to accommodate." Croves speaks with just the tinge of an accent. German, perhaps, or Dutch. I can't tell.

"Very gracious of you, sir," Huston says. "Naturally I am disappointed not to have met the man himself. I would have prized any suggestions he might have made regarding the screenplay."

"Bruno has read your screenplay which you were kind enough to send him and he is more than pleased by your adaption."

Huston smiles, raises his shot of tequila in a salute and downs it. As an afterthought he remembers I am sitting at the table and introduces me. Croves and I exchange pleasantries. When I ask him how he came to know Traven he is evasive and when I ask what sort of work he does, he generalizes about investing and money management. Huston, too, tries to draw him out but he doesn't have much to say about himself and keeps bringing the conversation back to Traven.

Another man appears in the doorway and the guard again bars the way. Croves leans in to Huston and says quietly, "My friend." Huston waves him in.

He is tall, burly and dark with tanned outdoorsy skin and jet black hair and a five o'clock shadow that leads me to believe that he has to shave at least twice a day. His name is Jose Herrera and he claims to be a free lance journalist with ties to several Madrid newspapers. He is not as smooth as Croves and there's something about him that smells of hired muscle. My suspicions are confirmed when I get a quick glance at a revolver in a shoulder holster when he sits.

"Expecting trouble?" I ask.

"Senor?"

"Most journalists I know carry a number two pencil, not a thirty-eight revolver."

He forces a smile. "The streets of any city can often be dangerous, Senor. In your country as well as here, I'd say," he says.

I nod. "And I'd say your duties include more than just chauffeuring."

Croves pipes up. "In this country, it is not a crime to carry a gun if you are properly licensed."

"Oh, I'm sure. It's probably also not a crime to pretend you are someone you are not," I say.

Croves and Herrera exchange a quick look. Croves looks back at me. "You are right, sir," he says. "Why I believe that your father, Senor Huston, is not using the name he was born with. And I say, where is the crime in that?" The smile is there but the eyes are colder than a polar bear's butt.

"Well, boys, enough of this name crap. Senor, what's your pleasure?" John says heartily.

Herrera orders a tequila but he and Croves both decline food when Huston orders lunch.

Croves sips his beer and then he says, "Bruno has heard disquieting rumors that some changes are to be made on the shooting script."

Huston shakes his head. "They are untrue."

"And the arrival of Miss Sheridan?"

"An inappropriate notion dreamed up by our associate producer who has yet to learn his place in things. I will assure you and you may assure Mr. Traven that this film will be an accurate and affectionate representation of the book he wrote twenty-one years ago. You have my word on that."

"And do I have Mr. Jack Warner's word on that?" Croves asks.

"Let me amend my statement," Huston says. "As long as I am directing this movie, nothing will change."

Croves smiles. "Then you will not mind if I visit your set during filming."

"I welcome it," Huston says.

We chat for a few more minutes with Croves and Herrera revealing little about themselves. Then they excuse themselves and leave. Huston stares after them thoughtfully.

"What?" I ask, curious about his expression.

"Like you, Joe, I'm just wondering why Mr. Traven would go to all this trouble to pass himself off as someone he's not?"

"But are you sure?" I ask.

"My young friend," he says, "I am positive."

CHAPTER FOUR

It's four o'clock when I finally get through to Henry Blanke at the studio. We are two hours later than the West Coast and he is just returning from lunch. He has a meeting in a few minutes so I don't waste time. I'm probably not being smart, I certainly am not doing the politically savvy thing, but if I don't know where I stand, I don't know how I can possibly get my job done. So I tell him about Phil Drago's cavalier behavior.

He hears me out and then he says, "Look, Joe. Phil can be a real pain in the ass but right now I feel sorry for him. Mr. Warner hates this picture. He hates the script, he hates the dailies and he's even beginning to hate John Huston which, in my opinion, is not a smart thing to do. Mr. Warner is giving me orders which I pass along to Phil to lighten up the film. It needs humor, it needs some sort of sex appeal. I mean, what we're looking at is grim and gloomy and frankly, Mr. Warner thinks we are throwing money down a rathole."

"But didn't he green light the picture?" I ask.

"Sure. He gave the go ahead and he knew it was a serious film but he never counted on something this serious. You know Jack. Give him Cagney in a gangster film or the new kid, Doris Day, in a musical and he's comfortable. With this he squirms through dailies and uses a lot of four letter words."

"Yes, but---"

"Joe, I'm trying to spell it out for you. Phil is speaking for Mr. Warner and for me but he can't let Huston know where it's coming from. You get it?"

"Okay, I understand the problem but from where I'm sitting, Mr. Huston seems to know exactly what he's doing and Phil hasn't a clue."

"Yeah, that's a problem," Blanke says. "Anyway, cut Phil a little slack, will you, Joe?"

"I'll do my best," I say and then add, "Oh, and Mr. Blanke, the author of the book has shown up on the set and he's made it clear he is concerned about how his novel is going to be treated."

"He is, huh?" Blanke says. "Well, screw him. We bought the rights, we do what we want. Gotta run, Joe. Keep in touch." And he hangs up.

I also hang up and I feel utterly depressed. A quiet war is being waged and I can feel myself being drawn into it. Well, I tell myself, that is not going to happen. This is between the producers and the director with possible kibitzing from the author and it is their business, not mine. I am not getting involved. Period.

Feeling much better about things, I decide I'll take a walk around town and check out the sights. Maybe I'll find an American hamburger stand, though I doubt it. I'd even settle for an Italian ristorante or maybe Chinese. Anything actually. Fajitas, tacos and burritos are fast becoming my least favorite foods.

I leave the hotel and head north toward one of the major plazas. As I do, I pass a Pemex gas station and I see Pedro Castano in animated conversation with Hal Croves' buddy, Jose Herrera, who is trying to fill the tank of his '39 DeSoto. Actually it's not so much a conversation as a shoving match. I can't tell what they're saying but it is pretty heated. I think about wandering over to break it up but then remember that I am no longer involved. We have what is known in movie parlance as an unhappy set. It's not the first, it's not going to be the last and it's none of my business. I leave Castano and Herrera to settle their problems themselves.

The plaza is a bust. In the center is a statue of a man whose name I cannot pronounce. He is astride his horse and I cannot remember if this means he died in battle or if he died in bed. I decide I don't care. A huge church dominates one side of the square. An open air market takes up another side. Business has slowed to a crawl. The mamacitas are all at home cooking the evening meal. There are the usual public buildings, a bank, a hotel (dining room menu features Mexican food) and three restaurants, all Mexican. I long for The Brown Derby.

I hear the shouts and squeals of young children off to my left and I go to investigate. I find a small public park where a dozen or so youngsters are involved in a high energy soccer game. I am amused to note that there is one adult playing along with them and his name is Tim Holt. Tim is 29 and in good shape but it's obvious he's having trouble keeping up with the little ruffians. After a few more minutes, he throws up his hands in defeat, tells the kids he's had enough and starts to walk toward me, sweat beading on his forehead and his breath coming in short pants.

He grins. "Nothing like a bunch of twelve year olds to let you know how old you're getting," he says.

"Not what I saw," I say.

"Then you need specs. I'm going to pay for this tomorrow," he says as he stretches. We start to walk back to the plaza. "You're the press guy," he says.

"Joe Bernardi."

"Tim Holt."

We shake.

"Have you met my Dad?" he asks.

"Not yet."

"He's got a small part. He's doing it to be with me. He really doesn't need it."

"I'm sure he doesn't," I say.

"I think he'd make a nice interview," Tim says. "You know he used to be big. I mean, very big."

"I know."

"One of the pioneers of the talkies. God, the credits that man has. But you know how this business is. They want you and then you get to be old hat and you have to step aside. It's kinda sad."

"I agree. But you know, he's still working."

Tim smiles. " You're right. He's stlll working." Tim stops walking. "Joe, do me a favor. Play me down. I want a low profile."

"Yours is a pretty big story, Tim. Years of working in B westerns, suddenly you get a break. Huston, Bogart, this is heady company for you."

"Yes, it is, and that's why I don't want to get hyped. You build me up to be something I'm not, it can only hurt. If expectations are low and I do a good job, that's the best I can hope for. Do you see my point?"

I do. Tim's got a head on his shoulders.

"I'll play it your way," I say. "And I'll chat with your Dad."

"Thanks," he grins. He checks his watch. "You heading back to the hotel?"

"Might as well," I say.

"Good. Let's go," he says. "I've got sort of a date with Annie tonight?"

"Sheridan?"

He gives me a 'Are you kidding?' look. "Joe, give me a break. I'm between wives."

"Go for it," I tell him.

I hurry straight to my room and catch Bunny still at her desk at The Reporter. She got the Bogie story into today's edition and Wilkerson is fawning all over her. Phineas and Harry Frakes both missed their deadlines. I'll hear about this later. She's happy and well and not planning to run off with the ad salesman any time soon. I tell her I wish she was here or that I was there, either way, and I mean it. When I hang up I consider myself done for the day unless a crisis arises and I decide to sit on the veranda and let the breeze from the Gulf wash over me as the sun goes down and I nurse a cold beer.

I am just settling in when Phil Drago emerges from the hotel lobby and makes a beeline in my direction. I can see he's not a happy man. As short as he is, he towers over me but only because I am sitting down.

"You talked to Henry," he says, every word an accusation.

"I did," I say.

"Are you out of your mind?" he wants to know.

"Don't think so," I say.

"I can have you thrown off this picture," he growls.

"No, you can't," I say pleasantly.

"Listen to me, Bernardi----"

"I can hardly help not listening to you. Keep your voice down. Your scaring the cucarachas."

"I am in charge on this set, not Henry Blanke---"

"You're wrong, Phil. You are carrying Henry's banner and so am I and we both answer to Henry, you no less than me. I plan to talk to him whenever and however I choose and you had better get used to the idea. Now Henry has told me the bind you're in and has asked me to cut you some slack which I am going to do, but starting now, you're going to stop throwing your weight around when it comes to my job. You sabe, Felipe?"

I look him dead in the eye and I can see him groping for a face saving response because now a half a dozen people nearby are staring at us.

"Now before I have to call Henry again, let's you and me talk about Jimbo Ochoa," I say.

"So he came whining to you," Phil says with a smirk.

"His wife's about to have a baby. Three days isn't much, Phil."

"I can't spare him."

"Sure you can."

"Look, he's a smart assed kid who doesn't know his place."

"Not by me. Why don't you pull that poker out of your ass and bend a little?"

"Anyway, Huston wants him here," Phil says.

"So now you're going to blame Huston. How about if I check with Huston directly?" I ask.

Again, he is trapped by another of his lies. He is saved by the arrival of a police car which pulls to a stop near the front steps and a beefy man in uniform gets out and lumbers up the steps towards us. He's jowly with bags under his sad looking eyes and he sports a full black mustache above his upper lip. But there is something in the way he moves that belies his unprepossessing manner. He wears a giant .44 caliber revolver on his hip and I am pretty sure he knows how to use it.

He smiles. "Senor Drago," he says.

"Chief," Drago says.

"I was expecting you at my office today as we discussed."

"Sorry, I got a little busy----"

The Chief overrides him. "And then when you do not show up, I say to myself, this is a very busy man and I must not inconvenience him so I get into my car and come to you."

"This is not a good time, Chief."

"If not now, then when, my friend? I can do nothing about El Jefe if you do not share with me your problems and bring charges against this man."

"I told you, our problems have been minor. We can handle these things ourselves."

"I don't think so, senor."

Nervously Drago glances at his watch. "I'm sorry, Chief, I have an important meeting. This will have to wait." And with that he turns and hurries into the hotel. The Chief watches him go, obviously troubled.

"He has a lot on his mind," I say.

He looks down at me warily.

"We have not met."

I introduce myself and invite him to sit down and have a beer. My treat. He shakes his head. He's on duty.

"Then sit down anyway," I say. "No chess lessons, I promise."

He sits and smiles. "You have been talking to Mr. Bogart," he says.

"I have," I say.

He is 51 years old. His name is Benito Santiago and he has been the Chief of Police in Tampico for the past thirteen years. It is an elected post and he is a very popular man. He has one wife, six children and two grandchildren and he loves his job. He says he does not love his job when people like Phil Drago prevent him from doing it. As he says this, his visage darkens and I can tell he regards this as a serious matter.

"Tell me about El Jefe," I say.

He pauses. "In Spanish, it means The Chief, but this man is not the Chief of Police, he is the leader of a group of worthless, shiftless lobos who prey on the good people of Tampico."

I take a guess. "Extortion, strongarm, blackmail, assault."

"And a few other things," he says.

"We have people like that in most of our cities."

"So I have been told." Santiago takes a small cheroot from his pocket and lights up. It smells like a dung heap. Belatedly he asks if I mind. Why should I mind? He's the one wearing the gun.

"Your Mr. Drago, he does not seem to understand. If you do not confront these people immediately, things only get worse. You hire thirty of our people, El Jefe wants ninety. He takes half what you pay each one. Ninety is more profitable than thirty."

"And no one complains?"

"They are afraid. He has good lawyers. He pays them well. Besides, even giving him half, this is a great deal of money for my people. No, they will not speak up."

I nod in understanding. "I think Mr. Drago is counting on the fact that the company will be moving to Durango early next week."

Santiago smiles wryly. "And does he think Durango will be any different? Word spreads, Mr. Bernardi. A few miles. A few hundred miles. The word is out. Mr. Drago is, how do you say it in your country, a pigeon? I am ashamed that people like El Jefe are all over my country. Durango will be no better than Tampico."

"So you're saying, stop him here. Make an example of him."

"That is what I am saying."

He gets to his feet and puts out his hand. "I am happy to meet you, senor. Buena suerte." We shake and then he heads for his car and drives away.

I sit there for a long time watching the sun disappear and the sky turn to a panoply of blue and salmon pink. I order a couple of more beers and I think this is my way of avoiding dinner hour which is pretty silly since the dining room is not scheduled to open for another forty minutes. I wonder if the chef would be insulted if I were to ask for a plain piece of broiled chicken and a green salad on the side. I muse about the origin of refried beans and wonder why they have to be fried twice. I try to get straight in my head the difference between a burrito, an enchilada and a tamale. I have no clue. I wonder if I wouldn't be smart just to go inside and order one of everything and see if I can discover one dish that will titillate, not torture, me.

My reverie is interrupted by the sound of applause coming from within. It is loud and it is sustained and my curiosity forces me to my feet. I step inside the dining room which is packed with people, not just the crew, but other guests and some people I have never seen before. Townspeople, I gather. Standing at one end of the room and backed by an unlikely trio of guitar, drums and bass fiddle is Walter Huston who has just quietly started to perform his famous rendition of 'September Song'. It is deathly still. All eyes are on this man of 64 years who introduced this beautiful melody 9 years ago in a Broadway musical called "Knickerbocker Holiday." I am mesmerized by his talent and his presence. There is a reason this man's career has endured for more than forty years. He is a star.

I let my eyes roam over the assemblage. Tim Holt is standing against the wall in the rear, his arm draped around Ann Sheridan's shoulders. A smooth operator, this man Tim. I look at Ann and the way she's looking at Tim. She's pretty smooth herself. Down front, Carlos Martinez, the Film Commission guy, is sitting crosslegged on the floor looking up at Huston in silent awe. I spot Hal Croves leaning against the wall, listening as intently as everyone else. It may be my imagination but I think I see moistness in his eyes. If, as John Huston believes, this man is really the writer-anarchist, Bruno Traven, the sentimentality he is showing seems very out of place. I sidle through the crowd and reach him as Huston finishes and the room again erupts in appreciative applause. Croves looks at me and nods with a little bob of the head. I ask if he will let me buy him a drink. He shrugs an assent and we head off to the bar.

Croves orders a margarita and I stick with a beer. The waitress brings a bowl of pretzels and I dig in thinking this may be a decent alternative to dinner.

"I'm disappointed I won't be meeting Mr. Traven," I say by way of opening the conversation. "I was hoping to tell him how much I enjoyed reading his book."

"I will pass your kind comments along," Croves says. He shakes some salt on the side of his hand, licks it and then takes a deep swallow from his glass. I always wondered why they didn't just shake the salt into the drink and be done with it.

"I'm curious, Mr. Croves. What sort of man is Mr. Traven? I know very little about him."

"He is not a social man. He keeps to himself. When he feels he has something to say, he writes it down and has it published."

"And how does he spend his days?" I ask. "Reading, gardening, hiking? Does he have any hobbies?"

Croves regards me curiously. "And why would you wish to know these things, Mr Bernardi? Is it not your job to publicize this film? What would that have to do with Mr. Traven's private life?"

"I thought I might write a story for release by the studio. World famous author visits movie set to watch filming of his most famous novel, chats with famed director, hobnobs with cast and crew."

Croves smiles. "Interesting. Obviously not a story you can write since Mr. Traven is not here." He meets my look and doesn't flnch.

"Well, he might show up. I never lose hope," I say.

"I can assure you, he will not be coming," Traven replies.

"You would know better than I," I say. "So is he working on anything new? A novel, maybe. Something I can write about it."

Croves smile fades. "I think he would prefer that you write nothing about him. As I said, he guards his privacy jealously."

"Fair enough. How about you, Mr. Croves? Tell me a little about yourself."

He shakes his head. "I, too, am a private person, Mr. Bernardi."

"And your associate, Mr. Herrera, he, too, would be a private person?"

"Very much so."

"Well, he obviously knows at least one other person here," I say. Croves lifts his head with a curious look. "Pedro Castano, the actor," I say.

"I don't think so," Croves says.

"Really? About two hours ago your friend and Castano were having a very heated discussion at the service station just up the road. Seemed to me they knew each other quite well, if not happily."

"I think you're mistaken. Jose was with me most of the afternoon, helping me with some research."

"Now that's odd," I say. "I could swear----"

Croves smiles. "It is a natural mistake we gringos make. How would you say it in your country, all Hispanics look alike? Not true, of course, but most Mexicans have similar hair and skin color. It is easy to mistake one for another."

He says it so smoothly that I almost believe him but then

I realize he is full of crap. It was Herrera, all right, but why is Croves trying to convince me it wasn't?

I take a long draught on my beer as I stare at this thin little man with the ice cold eyes and I wonder what his game is. Bruno Traven or Hal Croves, either way, this man arrived with an agenda but I haven't the slightest idea what it is.

CHAPTER FIVE

It is morning and I bound down the stairs because I have figured out what to do for breakfast. Two eggs, hard boiled, salt and pepper, one piece of toast, and two cups of coffee. If the chef can't handle that simple request, I will take over the kitchen, at the point of a gun if need be.

As I reach the lobby I spot Ann Sheridan at the desk and walk over to her. I introduce myself and she smiles in return. She is a vision in navy blue with a perky white straw hat nestled on her flaming red hair. I start to have envious thoughts about Tim Holt but immediately put them out of my mind.

"Checking out?" I ask.

She shakes her head. "Checking for messages. I may leave late this afternoon. John asked me to do a little on-camera walk-by, just as an inside joke. We're trying to figure a good place to do it."

"Then you won't be playing a love interest for Bogie?"

She smiles. "You know, I don't know whose bird brained idea that was but whoever it is, he ought to get out of the business."

Now I smile. "I think it came direct from Mr. Warner himself."

"Oh," she says thoughtfully. "In that case, you and I have never met and we never had this conversation."

"No, we did not," I say, "but even though we didn't, it's been a pleasure, Miss Sheridan."

"Thank you,--uh---" She gropes for my name.

I wag my finger and whisper. "We never met, remember?"

She chuckles and heads out the main entrance. I am about to go into the dining room when Jimbo Ochoa comes down the stairs and moves quickly to the desk. He hasn't noticed me.

"You're sure he left no messages?" Jimbo says to the clerk. He's obviously annoyed and he doesn't mind showing it.

"No, senor. No messages."

"His bed hasn't been slept in."

The clerk shrugs with a knowing smile. "Perhaps he found a bed elsewhere, senor."

"Not this man," he says and turns away and nearly bumps into me. "Sorry, Joe," he says.

"What's the problem?"

"Pedro Castano. I can't find him. I'd set up an appointment for him last night with a local doctor to take his physical and he never showed."

"And he's not in his room?"

"Or anyplace else I've looked," Jimbo says.

"Hospital? Jail?"

"Nada. Not even church where he goes every morning."

"Odd," I say.

"Actors," he mutters in disgust, as if that says it all.

He starts to walk away. I grab his arm.

"Jimbo, I talked to Drago." He looks at me hopefully. "He won't budge."

An angry look crosses his face. "The little bastard, I'd like to punch his lights out." And then his body sags a little, resigned. "Yeah. Well, thanks anyway, Joe."

"I can go over his head. Your call."

"Forget it," he says. "I'm no good to anybody if I go home without a job."

I nod. "I hear you. So where are we shooting today?" I ask.

Jimbo points. "A little pocket park about three blocks over. Mr. Bogart and Tim Holt. A whole lot of yackety-yack. We'll be there until at least lunch."

"I'll drop by soon as I eat," I say.

With great misgivings the chef has boiled me two 10 minute eggs. He first tried to sell me on an omelet with salsa and onions, chili peppers and spicy sausage on the side. When I picked up a meat cleaver, he gave in. Stomach full, I wander over to the set.

As usual the company has attracted a crowd but the security guys have kept them at a distance. Bogie and Tim are sitting on adjoining park benches getting to know each other. John Huston is squatting next to them, gesturing, and imparting some suggestions which both seem to agree with. Hal Croves is across the way smoking a cigarette. Although he's exceptionally well dressed, he doesn't look much like a movie star so the locals leave him alone.

I spot Walter Huston standing next to the sound engineer. He's wearing earphones which will enable him to hear the dialogue clearly via the boom mike when actual filming begins. I walk over and introduce myself. He smiles warmly and we shake. His grip is firm. His eyes are clear. Despite his ten day growth of beard and his tousled white hair, he belies his age. I tell him how much I enjoyed his singing the previous evening.

"Very kind of you, young man. Very kind. That show and that song have a special place in my heart."

"I'm not surprised," I say. I also tell him how much I enjoyed his performance in 'Yankee Doodle Dandy', playing Jimmy Cagney's dad.

He grins broadly. "Now there was a picture," he says. "I'd been badgering Jack and Harry and everybody else on the lot to give me a chance to twinkle my toes and exercise my pipes. Took them long enough to get around to it."

"It sure looked like you were having fun," I say.

"Well, that was Cagney," he says. "He made it a joy to come to work. A wonderful set. Wonderful cast. Should have been filmed in color. Lots of red, whlte and blue but the war came along and we couldn't get the film stock. Still and all, it turned out really well and Cagney, my God, if anybody deserved an Oscar it was him."

"I heard that Cohan himself thought he was perfect."

"You heard right, son," Walter says.

Suddenly I am aware of a murmuring in the crowd and people shuffllng about. I look up to see two cars pull to the curb, very close to the set. The first is a stunning 1935 12 cylinder white Packard formal sedan. No one pays much attention to the second one. John Huston stands up and Bogie and Tim turn to look as a gaunt looking man perhaps in his 30's gets out of the Packard and pauses, taking in his surroundings. There is a small but distinct scar alongside his left eye which droops badly as if in a permanent wink. He is wearing a light double breasted gabardine suit and a snap brim fedora and there is no question in my mind who this man is. Three men emerge from his car, three others from the second car. All six are wearing pistols on their hips.

Walter leans in close and half-whispers, "What? No Fredo?"

"Who's Fredo?" I ask.

"His brother. He never goes anywhere without him."

As the man walks toward the set, people move out of his way including the private security people hired for the duration of the shoot. He hardly seems to notice as his gaze looks everywhere.

Huston rises to intercept him.

"Can I help you?" Huston says.

"I don't think so," the man says . "I do not see Mr. Drago."

"He's back at the hotel," Huston says.

"I had hoped to see him here," the man says.

"This is a closed set and we're in the middle of filming so why don't you and your companions go elsewhere."

By this time Bogie and Tim have moved up behind their director and I force myself not to smile. That look in Bogie's eyes, I've seen it in a dozen films. He's itching for a brawl. I look at the American crew. They're not sure what to do, all except for Jimbo Ochoa who has inched forward and is intently studying the faces of the six men backing up El Jefe. The local Mexicans are inching backwards very cautiously. They know what they're dealing with.

"You know who I am?" the man says.

"I know and I don't care. Take your men and vamoose, Jefe. There's nothing here for you."

El Jefe smiles a mirthless smile. "I did not come to make trouble, Mr. Huston. I am an admirer of your films. The one about the black bird, it is one of my favorites. No, no. I came to offer my sympathies about the troubles you have been having. These incidents, they are a shame. So costly and so avoidable."

I lean in toward Walter and whisper, "I think your son could use a hand." The elder Huston grabs me by the elbow and holds me back. There's a twinkle in his eye.

"Johnny can take care of himself," he says.

And sure enough, Huston steps forward until he is right in the man's face. I'm too far away to hear every word because John is keeping his voice down but I think it goes something like this. Take your phony apology to Mr. Drago. I don't care. And if you are not off my set in thirty seconds I am going to fire all of your men that I hired and then I am going to call the federales in Mexico City and invite them up here for the next eight days to meet the stars, get drunk and watch the filming. Do I make myself clear?

Or words to that effect.

For a moment, no one moves and I wonder if John hasn't overplayed his hand. But at that moment I hear the wail of a police car approaching and the Chief's squad car pulls to a stop, boxing in El Jefe's car. Santiago gets out, hefts his gun belt and approaches.

"Do we have a problem here, Senor Huston?" he asks.

"I don't know. Do we?" John looks El Jefe square in the eye.

El Jefe considers his options and then shrugs. "A pleasant conversation, that is all. We were just leaving." He looks at Santiago and then toward the Chief's cruiser. "If you wouldn't mind moving your car, Chief."

Santiago stares him down, "I'll move it when I am ready to leave." They lock eyes and it is El Jefe who looks away with an amused smile. Santiago turns to John.

"I know the trouble this man is bringing to you. If you would like to press charges, Senor Huston, I think now is the time."

John nods. "You're probably right, Chief, but that's not a decision I can make. You'll have to talk to Phil Drago."

Santiago shrugs. "Yes, I have talked to Mr. Drago. It is like talking to my dog and expecting a reply." He shoots a dirty look toward El Jefe and then turns again to Huston. "I do not see Mr. Drago here."

"No, he's still at the hotel."

"I see. Then I will inform you. An hour ago, two boys who should have been in school were playing in the rock quarry outside of town and came across a dead body. All identification including the man's wallet was removed but from his dress and his grooming I know he is not local. I need someone to come with me and perhaps to identify him."

John hesitates as he looks around, scanning the crowd. "I know of no one missing, Chief, and frankly, we're in the middle of a scene and I can't spare anyone to go with you."

I hear this and step forward. "I'll go," I say.

John looks at me and nods gratefully. "Here's your man, Chief," he says.

"Gracias," Santiago replies and leads me toward his cruiser. He pauses for a second as he reaches El Jefe. He looks the bandit leader square in the eye.

"Do not test me, Jefe," he says. "I tell you this only once."

We climb into the squad car and drive away. I look back and watch as El Jefe and his men get in their cars and leave.

"You've got a pair, amigo," I say with a grin. Santiago looks at me blankly. "Cujones," I say.

He smiles. "Ah, yes. Cujones. Not to worry, Senor Bernardi. El Jefe rarely acts in broad daylight. He prefers moonless nights, dark alleys, and knives to the back."

"Still and all, he sounds like a dangerous enemy."

"Yes, and I tell you this. At night I lock up my house very tightly and then I sleep very quietly with my pistol under my pillow and I pray to Saint Anthony that this man will try to get into my bedroom to kill me. I pray for this so that Tampico will be rid of him once and for all. Comprende?"

"Si." I nod my head appreciatively. "Cujones grande."

"Gracias," Santiago says.

The rock quarry is not particularly big but it is active, though at the moment all work has ceased. I see a couple of squad cars parked at the foot of an access road next to a black van that I take to be the city meat wagon. A couple of uniforms and several men in civilian clothes are hovering around an area about twenty yards away where I think I catch a glimpse of the body lying face down on the ground.

We park and walk over. Two guys in suits are carefully checking out the area around the scene while another is examining the body. I take him to be the coroner. He and Santiago exchange greetings and then I am summoned as they turn the body over. I think I already know who I am going to be looking at but I am still taken aback as I peer down at the dead features of Pedro Castano. His face and head are battered and bloody and his hands are scraped and bruised. One of his legs is canted in a strange position and it appears to be broken. His clothing is dirty and torn. It seems cruel that this pleasant man who wanted only to perform for others and support his family should come to such a gruesome end. I think of his wife and family who I have never met. Their lives have been shattered, perhaps permanently. I'm glad I won't have to be the one to tell her.

"Yes, I know him," I say. "Pedro Castano. He's an actor with the film company."

"Ah," the coroner says. "I thought I knew his face. Castano. Yes, of course. Oh, this is sad. Very sad." He and Santiago speak English for my benefit.

"How was he killed, Chuy?" Santiago asks.

"Well, at first I thought it was the fall." He glances up to the main roadway about thirty or forty feet above us. The face of the cliff is rock strewn everywhere. "Then I spotted the entry wounds." He points them out. "Here and here. One to the belly, the other to the heart."

"Doesn't look like a lot of blood," Santiago notes.

"This is a dumping ground. He was killed somewhere else. I'd say whoever did this, drove the body to the top of the cliff and shoved him over. These cuts and bruises look post-mortem."

"And obviously no murder weapon," Santiago says.

"Your men are still looking but I doubt it. If and when they ever find it, it will have a long thin blade, maybe eight or nine inches long."

"Like a stiletto."

"Exactly."

Santiago continues to stare down at the body. "Even though his watch and wallet are missing, I do not think this is a case of robbery. Robbers do not go to the trouble of moving bodies." He turns to me. "We will take him to the morgue. Meanwhile, if you would be so good as to inform Senor Drago----"

"Of course I say.

"I will need to speak to everyone involved with the film company. I hope this will not cause delays in your work but it must be done. Perhaps if the crew could be gathered around five o'clock at the hotel---"

"I understand."

Santiago nods thoughtfully. "Frankly, I do not expect to find this man's killer among those working on the movie. I already have a good idea who is responsible."

So do I, I think to myself. But at that moment I do not tell the Chief that he and I suspect two entirely different people.

CHAPTER SIX

Santiago drives me back to the hotel. On the way I tell him about the confrontation I witnessed between Castano and Jose Herrera. Santiago has not yet met Herrera so I fill him in including what I know about Hal Croves, emphasizing the fact that he may actually be the author Bruno Traven. Santiago perks up. I can tell he's a man who loves intrigue because he asks me in detail my observations about both men. I do the best I can.

"I meant to ask you, Chief. About El Jefe. I was told he seldom goes anywhere without his brother Fredo. So where was he? Any idea?"

"I have heard," Santiago says, "that Fredo is not looking like himself today."

He glances at me with a sly grin and winks.

"Meaning?" I ask.

"Meaning that I have heard, though I have not seen, that Fredo's face looks as if it came in contact with an airplane propellor."

"You mean he got into a fight."

"If he did, I do not think he won it. I hear Fredo is home seeing no one until some of his cuts and bruises heal up. It would not do for El Jefe's brother to be seen in such condition."

I smile and lean back. Santiago catches my look of amusement.

"And perhaps you know something of this?"

"Perhaps," I say.

We fall silent for a couple of minutes. I am thinking back to that squabble at the gas station and kicking myself for not finding out what their disagreement was all about. I know this. Herrera was angry and so was Castano. But were the words enough the precipitate murder?

I realize Santiago is talking to me.

"I said, I wonder why your movie studio didn't just pay the money to El Jefe. I would not condone it but I have been told it's done all the time and is considered a small price to pay for peace on the location."

"I'm pretty sure that was a decision made by Phil Drago and by Drago alone."

"And his reason?"

"I think he wanted to prove how much in charge he was. He is not a bright man. I don't think he realized what he was up against but once he had committed, he probably felt he had no choice but to stick to his guns."

"I see," Santiago says, though I'm not sure he does.

"The studio head, Mr. Warner, is not happy with this film. Maybe Phil thought he'd be looking for any excuse to shut the picture down. I don't know. You really ought to ask Phil."

Santiago nods thoughtfully. "Yes, I think I will do that."

Once inside the hotel, I head straight for the production office and rifle through the casting files. I find the resume for Pedro Castano and slip it inside my shirt. If I'm going to answer questions about the victim it might behoove me to learn a little something about him. I start back to the lobby and fend off several reporters. I'm keeping mum until I get instructions from

L.A. That satisfies just about everyone but Phineas Ogilvy who dogs me all the way up the stairs to my room.

"Don't run, old top," he says. "I promise not to bite. Who's the stiff in the rockpile?"

"You'll have to ask Chief Santiago," I tell him.

"Tut tut, Joseph," he says, "that is no way to treat a fellow scrivener."

"Look, I told you, I'm calling the office for marching orders. If they say okay, I'll fill you in about fifteen minutes from now. Where's Harry?"

"He caught an early plane out. Poor fellow seems to be missing out on a very big story, wouldn't you say?"

I laugh. "I might say, Phineas, in about fifteen minutes. Meanwhile, buy yourself a beer. I'll see you in the bar."

Phineas does a sweeping Elizabethan bow and waddles off as I go into my room to chat with my boss, Charlie Berger.

I can tell that he's jealous.

"Thirty four years in this business and I never had a murder. You fall into one in less than a month. And that's not even counting what happened at Continental last year. 'Tain't fair, Joe." Charlie says.

"Sorry. You could always catch the next plane down here."

"Oh, sure, and I would only have to answer to my wife and my kids and my rabbi all of whom think I'm a feeble old man who should have retired five years ago. No, no, Joe, I'm envious but this is all yours and believe me, you are going to have your hands full."

"How so?" I ask naively.

"Because every prima donna reporter and columnist and radio personality in America is going to be descending on you like a shit storm. Each of these egotists is going to want all of your time, all of your inside information, and your absolute assurance that you are not helping any of their competitors in any way. Get the picture?"

"Yeah, sounds like fun. So what do I do?"

"Let it all hang out. Press conference twice a day. Hold nothing back unless the cops tell you otherwise and between conferences, no comment. They may not be happy with you but they won't crucify you either. If they catch you playing favorites, they'll tear you apart. Anything else I can help you with?"

I laugh. "No, that pretty much covers it. And Charlie, your rabbi is wrong. I don't think 84 is too old for this job."

"Fuck you," he says and hangs up.

I immediately call the Hollywood Reporter but Bunny's not in the office. I caculate the time difference and call her home number. No answer. I feel bad. This is going to be a big story and she's coming out of the gate last. I'll feel even worse if I find out she's been playing doctor-nurse with that ad salesman.

I look over at the bed where I tossed Castano's employment file. I take it to a chair by the window and start to leaf through it. It's pretty straightforward. Name, rank and serial number stuff, home address, phone contact in Mexico City, a couple of recent 8 x 10 glossies and a work resume that includes all his roles, exclusively in Mexican films. Then I notice something else. Just as he had told me, before he became an actor, he had been a detective with the metropolitan Mexico City police. I make a mental note to find out more about his years as a cop. It might have a lot to do with why he ended up face down in a rock quarry with two punctures in his gut.

I go downstairs and look for Phil. We have a murder on our hands and Phil is going to have to deal with it whether he likes it or not. I check the dining room, the bar (where Phineas is nursing a glass of wine), the rear of the hotel, the swimming pool area. He's nowhere in sight. Maybe he's hiding in his room. I ring him up. No answer. Maybe he's with the company though I doubt it. He seldom appears during shooting and with El Jefe on the loose, I would bet my last peso he's hunkered down where no one will think of looking for him. He will reappear only when he has to.

Phineas smiles as I approach, raising his glass. I'm pretty sure it's not his first. I tell him about the discovery of Pedro Castano's body and the gruesome way he died. I have no other details but I tell him it's a pretty good bet that the Times is going to be sending someone else down to Tampico to work the story.

"But I'm already here, old top," he says. "I need no assistance."

"And when was the last time you covered a murder?"

He ponders thoughtfully. "Either 'Kiss of Death' or 'Song of the Thin Man'. Can't remember which." Then, looking at me in mock surprise: "Oh, you mean a real murder." I nod. "Well, I must confess it was quite a while ago."

"How long a while?" I ask him.

He looks peeved. "Look here, Joseph, if you are going to get all wrapped up in petty details, we are not going to get anywhere."

"Tell you what, Phineas. Here's a little tidbit you might want to run with. A dozen years ago Pedro Castano was a cop. That might not be worth much but nobody has it except you. So call your paper, tell them what happened, tell them you have everything under control and you have me in your back pocket. That just might convince them to let you handle it."

"Excellent thinking, old top. I shall be in your debt forever. Or at least until next Tuesday. And now if you will forgive me," he says, pushing away from the table, "I have a phone call to make." He starts off and then turns back. "And Joseph, for the record, do I?"

"Do you what?"

"Have you in my back pocket?"

"We shall see," I say.

Phineas leaves and I go to the bar and order a beer. I take the bottle and wander out back to the pool area where I pick out a comfortable chaise. A half dozen kids are frolicking in the pool. A life guard is sitting atop his viewing platform ogling a bronzed blonde in a red bikini. If one of the frolicking little buggers should run into trouble in the next minute, he is on his own.

"Bernardi!" I recognize the voice. I turn as Phil Drago bears down on me like an out of control dump truck.

"Hi, Phil," I say, sipping my beer.

"I can't believe you're sitting out here, goofing off. We are in serious trouble," he says.

"Indeed we are."

"That son of a bitch, that El Jefe, still stirring things up, shutting down the set, sabotaging our equipment, God knows what he had to do with the death of Castano and worst of all, we are going to have to recast his part with hardly any notice."

I look at him in disbelief. "Worst of all? Jesus, Phil, have a little respect. The man is dead."

"I know that. I just meant---well, you know what I meant. This is just Godawful. When Mr. Warner finds out, it is going to hit the fan, mark my words, and they are going to blame me. That's right. Me. As if all this is my fault. Damn it, I am doing the best I can."

"I know you are, Phil," I say it so sweetly that he doesn't get what I mean.

"Have you talked to Henry?" he asks hopefully.

"No, I assumed you'd do that."

He nods, rubbing his hands together nervously. "Yes, I'd better." He glances at his watch. "This probably isn't a good time," he says.

"No time's a good time, Phil. Make the call."

He looks down at me, frowns, and then heads back into the hotel. If he's smart he'll call Henry right away because it's my guess that Charlie Berger has already told Henry what's going on. If Phil doesn't report in right away, Henry will have his scalp on his belt by sundown. Right now I believe the issue is not how smart Phil is but how dumb.

I lean back in the chaise, sip my beer and start to compete with the life guard for ogling privileges.

It hits the fan at 4:17.

Santiago had said he wanted the company assembled at 5:00 for questioning but now he is barreling through the door and heading for the registration desk. I've been chatting with John Huston who spent a half hour being berated by an unhappy Hal Croves. Croves was furious by a scene at the end of the movie where Curtin and Howard amiably part company. Croves says the scene does not exist in the book and paints a false upbeat ending to the moral of the novel. Huston argues that a light, optimistic ending is needed so that the audience doesn't leave the theater upchucking their popcorn and peanuts.

"Who won?" I ask him.

"Who do you think?" he asks me. "I'm the fucking director." He walks off as Santiago goes after the desk clerk.

"What do you mean, you can't give me that information?" he says. "You see this badge pinned to my shirt. That says you tell me what I want to know or I find you a nice quiet cell in the calabozo. You comprende?'

"Si," the clerk says. "The gentleman is in 208." Santiago grabs the key from the clerk's hand and as he starts for the stairs, he spots me. He waves to me to follow him.

We hurry down the second floor corridor to number 208. "I want you with me," he says, "so if I find anything, I don't get accused of planting evidence." He puts the key in the lock and swings the door open. We go inside.

"Whose room is this?" I ask.

"Jaime Ochoa, one of the assistant directors," he says.

"You have to be kidding, Chief. Anybody but Jimbo."

"A call came in about a half hour ago. A concerned citizen saw Ochoa leaving the rock quarry at daybreak this morning."

"I don't suppose he left a name," I say sarcastically, "like Captain America or Eddie Rickenbacker or Popeye the Sailorman."

"Anonymous," Santiago replies as he starts to check the closet, then the night stand next to the bed.

"Chief, I know this man. He wouldn't hurt anyone, believe me."

"Please relay that information to El Jefe's brother Fredo," Santiago says. He's got the mattress off the bed now and then drops to his knees to look under the bed. "I am not so badly informed as you might think, Senor Bernardi."

"That's a different case. He caught two men sabotaging the catering truck and he used his fists, not a knife."

"I think for an army Ranger fists are more than enough to do damage. I also have been told they are expert in the use of a knife."

"So's a teenager from East L.A.. What does that prove?"

Now he is pulling out the drawers of the dresser. When he gets to the bottom one, he pulls that one out as well and there, lying on the floor under the dresser, is a blood covered needle-like knife. He looks up at me and then takes a folded paper bag from his jacket pocket and opens it up. Carefully he places the knife in the bag.

"This is all wrong, Chief," I say. "This is an obvious frame up."

He nods. "Perhaps so. I agree this is all very convenient."

"What about the argument I saw between the victim and Croves' buddy Jose Herrera?"

Santiago shakes his head. "I talked to Senor Croves. He says Senor Herrera was with him all afternoon."

"Yeah, that's what he told me and it's a damned lie."

"Perhaps so. Or perhaps you were mistaken."

"No, I was not mistaken."

"I will tell you what bothers me more than your so-called argument and it is this. I wonder, where is this Jaime Ochoa you call Jimbo. No one remembers seeing him after the lunch break. This is strange for a man who has duties on the set. Would you agree, Senor Bernardi?"

"Yes, I would but you are wrong about him being a killer."

"We shall see. Meanwhile I am having the roads watched, the airport, the train station and the bus terminal. There is nowhere he can go that we will not find him." He walks to the door and opens it. He turns to me. "Coming?"

I nod and follow him out.

The lobby is full of people, cast and crew ready for their five o'clock interrogation. Santiago pulls Huston aside and tells him it won't be necessary. Then he goes to the desk and tells the hotel manager that at six o'clock he wants to talk to every employee that was on duty during the midnight to eight graveyard shift. Every employee, without exception, he says. A police car will be sent for anyone who does not show up. My guess is he's looking for somebody who saw Jimbo coming or going from the hotel in the hours just before sunup.

And then Santiago makes the easiest arrest of his long career in law enforcement. Jimbo Ochoa walks in the front door of the hotel, a 35 mm camera around his neck, somewhat puzzled by the crowd that has gathered. Santiago spots him and inside of thirty seconds, Jimbo is handcuffed. A minute later he is in the back seat of a squad car headed for the city jail.

CHAPTER SEVEN

've gone to my room just to get away from the crowd. All I want is a little quiet so I can put my thoughts in order. Room service has brought me a pot of coffee and I know I will regret drinking it later on when I try to sleep but sleep is the last thing on my mind. I start to make a list of things that will need to be done. Charlie's given me plenty of advice in dealing with the press but I have another problem. Phil seems to be totally incapable of handling anything. How much of his ineptitude is going to fall on my shoulders, I have no idea.

And then it comes to me. Has anyone notified Luisa Castano of her husband's death? It's Phil's responsibility but knowing Phil, it would never occur to him. Santiago might have made the call but that's a longshot. He's been busy. If she hasn't been notified there's a chance she'll hear it on the radio or read it in the paper. I can't let that happen so I get her number from the production office and dial her at her home in Mexico City.

She picks up after the second ring.

"Mrs. Castano?"

"Yes?"

"My name is Joseph Bernardi. I'm calling from the movie company at Tampico."

"Oh, yes," she says.

"Mrs. Castano, I don't know quite how to tell you this but early this morning----"

"I know," she says.

"You know?"

"A good friend of myself and Pedro is working with the construction crew. He called me just an hour ago."

There is weariness and sadness in her voice and I suspect she is all cried out. "I am so sorry. I did not know your husband well. In fact we just met yesterday but we talked a great deal and much of it was about you and how proud he was of you and how happy he was in his marriage."

"You are most kind, Mr. Bernardi. Pedro was a good provider and a good husband and a wonderful father to his daughters. Ours will be a lonely life without him but we will manage."

"I am sure," I say. "I just want you to know that we, all of us, will help the authorities in any way we can to find out who did this. You have my promise on that."

"Thank you," she says. "Senor Bernardi, can you tell me please when I will be able to claim my husband's body?"

"I really don't know," I say. "The law requires an autopsy. It may be a day or two. I can find out."

"That would be most kind," she says.

"And if there's anything else you need, anything I can do, please call me." I give her the number for the hotel and my room number and I spell my name for her. Again I express my condolences and hang up. I have done what had to be done but I feel inadequate. Words are just words. I have said the right ones. But words from a stranger have very little meaning.

It takes me until nearly ten o'clock but I finally get in to see Jimbo Ochoa and that's only because Chief Santiago has developed a tenuous bond with me. Phil Drago never got past the booking desk and the guy Martinez from the film commission huffed and puffed for nearly a half hour while his self-important threats fell on deaf ears. Around nine o'clock the studio had sent in a local lawyer who was told to come back in the morning. As Santiago put it, "I do not want my interrogation thwarted by a well-dressed bandido carrying a 200 peso briefcase".

Jimbo looks good and there are no bruises that I can see. When I am let into his cell he is having a bowl of abondagas soup with bread on the side. He smiles up at me gratefully.

"Hey, Joe, nice to see you."

"How are they treating you, Jimbo?" I ask.

"Aside from the bullshit arrest, I'm okay. Food's good. The Chief asks a lot of questions but so far no rubber hose."

"I think he's a pretty good guy. I also think he'll give you a fair shake."

"Thanks, Joe, but what the hell am I doing here? That actor Castano is dead and I'm supposed to have killed him with some kind of knife? I mean, that's crazy. I didn't even know the guy."

"You came looking for him this morning at the hotel. You were angry. You even went up to his room."

"Because he missed the damned doctor's appointment. I was getting tired of chasing after him."

"I believe that. But Chief Santiago might think you were using that as a way of deflecting suspicion from yourself once the body was found."

"That's a load of crap," Jimbo says. I can hear the anger rising in his voice. "Jesus, Joe, how stupid does he think I am? I'm supposed to have killed this man and then leave a bloody knife under the dresser for the housekeeper to find the next time she cleans?"

"You don't have to convince me," I say.

"Well, I'm sure as hell gonna have to convince these cops. Katey's back home going through God knows what and I'm stuck in this fucking jail cell. I swear to God, Joe, when I find the guy that planted the knife on me, I am gonna kill the son of a bitch with my bare hands."

"Take it easy," I caution."You let them hear you talk like that, you'll never get out of here."

"Yeah, yeah, you're right." He's up and pacing now like a caged animal.

"So where were you after lunch?" I ask.

He glares at me. "What's that got to do with anything?"

"I don't know. I'll tell you after you answer my question. You disappear from the set. You tell no one and no one knows where you are. People like Santiago are wondering why."

He pauses, then holds up his hands displaying his scabs. "You know about this."

"I do."

"When I came upon those two guys, I'd never seen either of them before and I sure had no idea one of them was El Jefe's brother. Anyway, yesterday when we broke for lunch, I was getting tired of the third rate catering the studio was paying for so I wandered down the street to this little cafe. I was about to go in when I spot the number two guy sittting at a table eating. I know it's him because of the black eye I gave him and the cut on his jaw which he's bandaged up. So, I'm trying to think of what to do. Maybe I'm nuts. Maybe I think I'm Dick Tracy but I get this crazy idea if I can follow this guy and he hooks up with El Jefe and I can get a picture of it, we have something we can bring to the police to put an end to all these work stoppages. Anyway I hotfoot it back to the set, tell Ken I need a still camera from the equipment trailer and he gives me a 35 mm loaded and ready to shoot. By the time I get back to the cafe the guy is leaving."

"So you follow him."

He nods. "To the barber shop, to the market where he buys a bunch of flowers and then finally to this house which I don't know anything about but later I figure is a whorehouse. I've already taken two or three good pictures of him alone but nothing with El Jefe or even one of his men."

"So you wait and wait----"

He nods . "And then around four thirty he comes out and a car comes by and picks him up. I'm quick enough to get a shot of the car as it goes by but since I'm on foot, that's the end of my surveillance. I go back to the set and nobody's there so I go to the hotel."

"Did you tell this to Santiago?" I ask.

"Sure. He asks me a dozen times what I was doing and I answer him a dozen times. Look, you're right. He seems like an okay guy. Thank God I'm not in the back room of some jail in L.A."

"How about last night? Where were you and what were you doing?"

"I was working in the production office until midnight preparing the call sheets for the morning,. Then I went to my room, fell into bed and went to sleep. I was out cold until six o'clock when my alarm went off."

"You never left the room?"

"Dead asleep, Joe. I swear. Can I prove it? No. Look, I've been straight with you and the Chief about everything. That's all I can do."

"Good. Keep to that story," I say. "I don't think they can make any of this stick. You'll probably be out tomorrow."

He smiles. "Nice to hear you say it, Joe."

I find Santiago in his office, paring his fingernails. He looks up at me, lazily arching an eyebrow.

"So, did you get my confession for me?" he asks.

"He didn't do it and you know it," I say.

He shrugs. "Maybe yes, maybe no."

"He told you why he was missing from the set all afternoon."

"Si."

"He has a couple of photos of one of the men who were vandalizing the studio truck. Doesn't that tell you something?"

"I will have the film developed first thing in the morning but even if it is true and there is a photo of one of El Jefe's men, this has nothing to to with the killing of the actor the night before."

Of course, he's right. I try another tack.

"Anybody could have planted that knife in his room. All of us keep our windows open. The locks on half the doors in the hotel don't work. It's a second story man's paradise."

"Es verdad," he says, nodding sagely. "And as you said, Senor, he does not have to use a knife, his fists will do as well. But you also pointed out correctly that many people are skilled with a knife, even these gang members from, where did you say, East Los Angeles?"

"That's right."

"Do you know, perhaps, where Senor Ochoa was born and brought up?" He picks up a piece of paper from his desk and scans it carefully. It looks like a radio fax.

I am mousetrapped. "East L.A.?" I venture.

"Si. And I am thinking it was not such a good place to be raised." He shakes his head sadly as he reads. "Shoplifting. Assault. Petty theft. Destruction of property. All of this before he is sixteen. No, this is not a place I would like to raise a child."

"Okay, so he's got a juvenile record," I say. "Did you also know that he served his country with distinction in the military with a few medals to prove it."

He nods. "That is in his favor," he says.

"Tell me, Chief, have you been able to figure out what sort of motive he had?"

"Not yet. If there is one, I will find it."

"And meanwhile?"

His face darkens and I see the steel in his eyes that belie his gentle folksy exterior. "And meanwhile, your friend stays in my jail."

"But---"

"Save me your buts, Senor Bernardi. At great embarrassment to me, someone in your organization, I suspect Mr. Drago, has notified the policia federale in Mexico City and I have been told to expect at least one and perhaps several representatives of the government the first thing in the morning."

"Dumb fuck," I mutter.

"Yes, even I know that expression. So you see, Senor Bernardi, now that the federales have been brought into this case, I must operate by the book and, as you Americanos would say, dot my 'i's and cross my 't's."

"You're sure it was Drago?"

"A strong suspicion."

"What about Carlos Martinez, the toadie from the film commission?"

"He was most adamant that this matter could be handled in Tampico. I think perhaps he doesn't like government interference any more than I do." Santiago gets up from his desk and leads me to the door. "I know how you feel about your friend, but with the government involved, anything can now happen.

As my people say, que sera, sera. Whatever will be, will be. Pray for the best."

He claps me on the shoulder and I leave.

It's almost eleven o'clock but the hotel dining room is still serving late supper. I'm not hungry so I head straight for the desk to check for messages. There are six of them altogether, two from Charlie and one from Bunny. I feel a hand drop on my shoulder and I turn. It's Bogie.

"How's the kid?" he asks.

"They're treating him okay," I say.

Bogie nods. "Santiago seems like an okay guy," he says. "Hard to believe the kid had anything to do with Castano's death."

"He didn't."

"Good to hear. What's with tomorrow? Are we shooting or what?"

"I don't know. What does Phil say?"

"Phil says nothing because nobody knows where he is. The last I heard he was waiting for guidance. He didn't say whether it was the Divine variety or just marching orders from the studio."

"No call sheet?"

"None I've seen. I think Tim and I are supposed to beat the crap out of Bart MacLane tomorrow. Wait. Let me amend that. Our stunt doubles beat the stuffing out of his stunt double. Mostly I'll be sitting around shooting the breeze with Walter and waiting for the sun to go down."

"I can't help you, Mr. Bogart. I really don't know."

Bogie nods. "The reason I ask, there's a rumor going around we might shut down for a few days and I could hop a plane back to L.A. to see Betty." Betty is his wife, Lauren Bacall. No one who knows her calls her Lauren.

"Maybe she could fly down here for a few days," I suggest.

Bogie shakes his head. "She's expecting in early January. The doc says flying is out." He hesitates. "Forget I told you that. No press until it can't be avoided."

"My lips are glued shut," I tell him.

"Good lad," he grins and walks off.

As I head for the stairs one of the waiters walks by and I tell him to bring up a couple of cold ones and a bowl of peanuts. I hustle to my room and make myself comfortable at my desk. My first call is to Charlie Berger who said to call him at home any time I get in, no matter how late. The message memos list six reporters who will be arriving tomorrow. On the phone he gives me five more. United Press was going to send Walter Kronkite but this afternoon they sent him off to Nuremberg to cover the trials. One of their new kids will be taking his place. Ring Lardner Jr. may also show, probably to see if there's a screenplay in the offing. It's been years since Ring was an actual journalist.

"I want you to treat these people with kid gloves, Joe. The best of everything. Champagne and fruit baskets in their rooms. Booze on the dresser. Hookers if they want 'em. If they have trouble finding a room, find one for them. I expect Warners to come out of this smelling like gardenias."

"Gotcha," I say. "What do you know about shutting down tomorrow?"

"Nothing. What does Phil say?"

"Phil's playing hide and seek," I tell him.

"Dumb son of a bitch," I hear him mutter. "I'll call Henry. He's not going to like this."

"Whatever you can do, Charlie. We're hanging out here like skivvies on a clothesline in a hurricane."

"Will do."

"Oh, and Charlie, one other thing. Castano. His file says he was a police officer before he took up acting. That was maybe twelve years ago. It's a long shot but could you see if anybody's got anything on his career as a cop. Can't research it here because my Spanish is about as good as my Swahili."

"You're right. That is a long shot but I'll see what I can find out."

I hang up and call Bunny. She picks up on the first ring.

"Thanks for the scoop," she growls, assuming correctly that it's me.

"I called your office and I called your home. No answer. Where were you? I don't know. I am not Dunninger, that so-called radio mindreader."

"Okay. You're right. Sorry," she says contritely. "You got anything I can use for tomorrow?"

"Nothing solid enough to print. Look, Bunny, why don't you hop a plane? This is big but I have a feeling it's going to get bigger."

"Billy won't go for it," she says.

"Tell him Variety's sending their best guy."

"He won't believe it."

I pick up one if the message slips. :"I got it right here, straight from Skigie Silverman. The guy's coming tomorrow and Skigie's putting him up at the Tampico Majestic Hotel."

She whistles. "Very fancy."

"Nothing too good for Variety," I opine.

"Okay, I'll ask."

"Tell him the room's free because you'll be bunking in with me."

"You have a jaded opinion of my virtue," she says.

"A woman as hot blooded as you has no virtue, my little chickadee." I've given her my best W.C. Fields.

She comes right back at me with Mae West. "A man that cocksure had better be very sure about his cock."

Is it any wonder that I love her? Beauty, brains and the filthiest mouth south of the Canadian border. I freeze. I consider calling her back. I forgot to give her the Castano-as-cop angle that I'd passed on to Phineas. Oh, hell, I think, if she comes I'll fill her in. If she doesn't it's her loss.

I finish up my calls. It's twelve thirty when I lay down on the sheets, window wide open and a soft breeze wafting across the room. I think about the nine hotel rooms I am going to have to book first thing in the morning and I think about Phil Drago, holed up somewhere, hoping that all the snafus will sort themselves out. But most of all I think of Jimbo Ochoa sitting in that jail cell , framed by a creep or creeps unknown and I make a silent vow to do something about it. War heroes should not be treated so shabbily.

CHAPTER EIGHT

I am awakened by a knock on my door. The sun is up but I can tell it's very early. I stumble out of bed wearing nothing but my skivvies and check my watch which I leave on my dresser every night before retiring. It reads 7:22. Considering everything that's going on, this could be anyone including Ann Sheridan so I slip on a robe before opening the door.

Jose Herrera appears to be about to knock again. He lowers his hand. "Senor Bernardi, I need a moment," he says.

I'm wary. "This really isn't a good time," I say but before I can shut the door he barges his way in and closes the door behind him. Suddenly I am very nervous. I wonder if I should shout out, but what would I shout? Intruder? Thief? Mugger? Fire?

"I have been told," he says, "that two days ago you witnessed me in some sort of confrontation with the murder victim."

"Mr. Croves wasted no time," I say.

"And I take it that because of this, you think I may have had something to do with the man's death."

"I never said that."

"But you imply it," Herrera says. He takes a couple of steps toward me. I try not to back up but it isn't easy. My bed is in the way.

"I implied nothing," I say. "It was an observation, that's all."

"And what were Senor Castano and I arguing about?"

"I don't know. I couldn't hear."

"So it could have been the weather."

"It wasn't the weather," I say. I am beginning to be annoyed by this man who crashed into my room uninvited. "I think you had better leave, Mr. Herrera. I have a busy morning ahead of me."

"It will wait," he says. He walks over to the window and looks out over the water. "You have a nice view here."

"Okay. If not the weather, what?"

"That really is none of your business," he says, "but since I have nothing to hide, I am going to tell you what our silly argument was about. Very simply, Mr. Castano thought he knew me from many years ago. He claimed I was some person I was not. I explained that he was mistaken. He refused to believe me, in effect, calling me a liar. I do not take kindly to people who question my honesty. The confrontation became more heated. Eventually I got in my car and drove away. That was the last time I saw him. And now I would appreciate it if you would drop the matter and stop talking about me behind my back."

He starts for the door.

"Who did he think you were?" I ask.

He stops and looks at me. "That is of no importance."

"When was this that Castano thought he knew you, Mr. Herrera? When he was a police officer?"

"I know nothing of that," he says.

"Because if it was, then I think his recollection of you might be of great importance."

"You are wrong, Senor. It was a case of mistaken identity, nothing more." He goes to the door and opens it.

"Maybe we should let Chief Santiago decide that."

He stares at me hard and there is danger in his eyes. "If I were you, I would do my best to leave the police out of this."

"Is that a threat?" I ask.

He doesn't answer. He goes out, shutting the door behind him. Now I know for sure that his argument with Castano was important and maybe even relevant to his murder. This conversation is something Santiago needs to know about right away.

A short while later I am in the lobby talking to the manager. The night before I had booked the remaining three vacancies and was told there would be checkouts this morning. The manager shakes his head regretfully. The few non-crew guests are staying put. The murder of Pedro Castano is bringing out the voyeur in everyone. In short, the circus is in town and everybody's looking for a front row seat. I ask the manager if he would check some of the other hotels in the city for me. He regrets to tell me that, they too, are completely booked. There might be availability at one or two of the motor courts on the outskirts of the city but these are not the sort---. Before he can finish I tell him to book everything he can find up to a dozen rooms. Warners will guarantee payment. He starts to protest but I tell him to save his breath. I am going to need those rooms even if they are dingy, hot and crawling with bugs.

I start toward the dining room where I can faintly hear John Huston addressing the crew and from what I can gather, the picture has been temporarily shut down. As I pass the cocktail lounge I see a solitary figure sitting at a small table in the middle of the room. It's Phil Drago, he's hunched over nursing a cup of coffee and he looks like hell.

I take the seat across from him. He looks up with bleary bloodshot eyes.

"What's going on?" I ask.

"Shut down," he says.

"So I gather. Your idea?"

"Police Chief. He got orders from this guy who's up from Mexico City."

I nod. "Where were you last night, Phil?"

"Out partying," he says.

"With who?"

"With me." He sips his coffee. "Did you know some of the cantinas in this city stay open until four o'clock in the morning?"

"Were you able to find all of them?" I ask.

"I tried," he says. He sips more coffee. "Henry's on his way."

"About time," I say.

He shoots me a sour look.

"Don't pout, Phil. This is good for you. Takes the pressure off. Why don't you try to get some sleep?"

"Tried. Can't."

I nod and get up. No sense chatting. He's oblivious. I leave him to his misery.

The dining room is still crowded but Huston has finished speaking. The crew members are forming little groups and chatting among themselves. I can tell from the buzz what they're saying. Is this it? Are we shut down for good? Are we going home? Is anybody back in L.A. hiring?

Phineas Ogilvy grabs me by the arm, a broad smile on his face.

"Your suggestion was brilliant, old top," he says. "They are leaving this story to yours truly. No additional help need apply."

"Excellent, Phineas, I'm sure you will do a fabulous job."

"Unquestionably," he says. "And now if you would be kind enough to give me an address for this El Jefe person----"

I look at him in disbelief. "No, no, Phineas. That is not a good idea."

"And why not, pray tell?"

"Because El Jefe is a very dangerous man," I tell him.

"And I am a journalist," he says firmly, puffing himself up. "I am protected."

"Not from El Jefe, you're not."

"He wouldn't dare use violence against a member of the press."

"Phineas, you are not back in Los Angeles. This is the real world and El Jefe is not a movie character being played by Thomas Gomez. The knife he carries is not rubber and the gun in his pocket is not loaded with blanks. Now, why don't you start your coverage at a more modest level?"

"And what would that be?" he asks, somewhat in a snit.

"For starters, I'm holding a press conference today at noon."

He glowers. "Sorry, old top, but I do not plan to write this story using handouts from Warner Brothers publicity department."

"Suit yourself."

"Joseph, you disappoint me. Despite your promise, right now my back pocket in which you are supposed to be residing feels very, very empty." He turns and shuffles off, still in a snit.

The room is starting to thin out when I catch up with Carlos Martinez, the grand poobah from the film commission.

"Ah, Senor Bernardi, good morning," he says effusively, shaking my hand.

"Well, I'm not sure how good it is, Mr. Martinez, considering we have temporarily shut down."

He puts on a properly concerned face. "Yes, but temporarily, I think that is the key. I am sure everyone will be back to work tomorrow morning."

"Tell me, sir, am I still considered a visiting dignitary?"

"But of course," he says. "Whatever I can do for you, consider it done."

"How about a dozen rooms in the best hotels inTampico?"

His face falls. "Ah, my friend, anything but that. I myself have tried to book accommodations for several of my colleagues on the commission who wish to come to help out." He sniffs the air. "As if I needed such help. No, I am sorry, Senor Bernardi. Anything else but I am afraid there are no rooms to be had anywhere in the city. I am most sorry," he says. A nod of the head and he goes off.

I'm disappointed but I pride myself on recognizing Mr. Martinez for what he is, a self-aggrandizing bag of hot air.

There's not much more I can do here at the hotel. I post a notice on the hotel's Activities Board announcing the noon press conference and then I get one of the crew to drive me to police headquarters . When scheduling a news conference it is helpful to actually have some news to impart so I am hoping that Santiago can update me on developments.

There's no one on the desk so I head down the hallway to his office door, rap twice and open it. I catch him talking to a suave looking gentleman in an exquisitely tailored silk suit.

"Sorry," I say, backing out.

"No, no, Senor Bernardi. Come in, por favor," Santiago says waving me back into the room.

I step inside as the man in the suit rises. He is tall and slim with a pencil mustache and black hair, parted in the center and slicked back. His white shirt is crisply starched, his tie is a Countess Mara and his shoes look like custom made alligators. If this is the guy from Mexico City, the government pays its people well.

Santiago introduces me. His name is Miguel Iglesia and he is, as I suspected, a captain in the policia federale. We shake. His grip is firm and his hand is cool and when he looks into my eyes, I can see him reading every dirty little secret I have kept hidden for the past twenty-eight years. All this while he smiles warmly.

I sit in a nearby empty chair and ask Santiago if he has had a chance to develop the roll of film that Jimbo took yesterday. Immediately Iglesia raises a cautionary hand.

"I do not think it wise to share police business with outsiders, Chief Santiago," he says.

Santiago shrugs."Senor Bernardi is not totally an outsider, Captain. He has been most helpful."

"Nevertheless----"

I jump in. "Look, I don't want to cause trouble here. I have a press conference scheduled for noon to fill in the reporters on what is happening. I do this rather than have them come over here and bother you at all hours of the day. But if you don't want my help, that will be fine with me. I really don't need the aggravation of mollycoddling dozens of loud, obnoxious, self-centered egomaniacs." I get up from my chair. "So, again, sorry to bother you, Chief. You know where to find me." I start for the door. I can see the Chief and Iglesia exchange looks.

"Momento." Santiago says. "I think we would be very grateful for your help, Senor."

I hesitate, looking from Santiago to Iglesia. I wait.

"Please. Sit down, Senor Bernardi," Iglesia says. He struggles to be gracious.

I sit. Chalk one up for the press agent.

Santiago answers my question about the photos that Jimbo took. The second man that Jimbo beat up is named Chulo Batista and it is said he works for El Jefe. Also the car which picked him up is owned by another man who, it is also said, works for El Jefe. But what does this prove? Nothing. El Jefe has no employment contracts. His orders are verbal. There is no paper trail and if Jaime Ochoa were to go into court and accuse El Jefe's brother and Chulo Batista, it would be their word against his. Two to one and the one is a gringo.

"Come on, Chief," I snort. "You know this Chulo is involved."

"Of course," Santiago says. "But we need proof, Senor Bernardi. Solid proof."

"What have you got on the knife?" I ask Santiago but Iglesia answers.

"The blood type on the blade is the same as the victim. The forensic examiner is 95% sure the wounds were made by the knife."

"Fingerprints?" I ask.

"All smudged. Nothing usable."

"Did the Chief tell you about the argument I witnessed between Castano and this man Jose Herrera?"

Iglesia shrugs. "Men argue," he says. "It seldom leads to murder."

"Is that right? Well, the man barged into my hotel room early this morning and threatened me. Is that also something that seldom leads to murder?"

Iglesia frowns. I can see that I have piqued his interest. He asks the nature of the threat. I tell him.

"And just who is this man Herrera?" Iglesia asks.

"He's a friend of a man named Hal Croves, both from Mexico City, and we don't know a hell of a lot about either one of them except that Croves might be the author of the book the movie is based on."

"But not using his real name."

"That's right."

"Interesting," Iglesia says thoughtfully. "I think perhaps I shall have a talk with both these men." He looks at me with a smile. "You have been helpful, Senor Bernardi. Anything else you think might be of use to us?"

I shake my head.

We spend the next few minutes discussing what information I can divulge at the press conference and what I should withhold.I'm probably being suckered but I begin to think that Iglesia might be a pretty sharp guy despite the showy wardrobe.

By the time I get back to the hotel it's nearing noon. I've got enough for my first press conference which will be attended by an audience of four. Phineas, of course. The guy from El Sol de Tampico, the local daily, and two guys from the Mexico City morning papers. Happily I've been told everyone speaks English. The bulk of the press corps will be arriving late this afternoon or early in the morning. Tomorrow I fear I will be dealing with as many as twenty surly and suspicious inquisitors.

I stop by the desk for messages and find a radio fax from Charlie Berger back at the studio. I tear open the envelope and read:

> To: Joseph Bernardi c/o Hotel Paloma Blanca,
> Tampico, Mexico.
>
> From: Charles Berger, Warner Brothers Studios,
> Burbank, California.
>
> Re: Former Mexico City police detective Pedro
> Castano.

Only one archival reference from L.A. based Spanish language newspaper. Twelve years ago, summer 1936. Violetta Munoz, daughter of highly placed official in Mexican government found dead of drug overdose in hotel room. Foul play suspected. Pedro Castano lead detective for metropolitan police force. Coroner finding accidental overdose. Father Armando Munoz dead of suicide following year. No other details.

I re-read the fax and I am very curious and also very troubled. Twelve years ago, the exact time when Castano resigned from the police force and took up a career in acting. Coincidence? Maybe. Maybe not.

CHAPTER NINE

My press conference at noon is short and to the point.

I describe the murder scene, the condition of the body, the blood on the knife, the absence of fingerprints and the lack, at least so far, of any other forensic evidence. When questioned about suspects, I say that the police are interrogating a company crew member but formal charges have not been filed. In fairness, I refuse to divulge his name though I'm pretty sure they already know it. I also say that Chief Santiago is following up on several leads. I verify that Captain Miguel Iglesia of the policia federale has been invited to assist Chief Santiago in his investigation. At the conclusion, no one throws ripe fruit or bandies obscenities in my direction. The local reporter even thanks me. I suspect this sort of unbridled support will not last long.

What do I not talk about? I do not tell them that it is possible, maybe even probable, that El Jefe and/or his brother murdered Pedro Castano and framed Jimbo Ochoa out of revenge for his interference in their extortion activities against the studio. Their message is blunt and unassailable. Get in our way and you pay the price. The imponderable is, why kill Pedro Castano? He seems to have no connection to El Jefe. Or was he just a victim chosen at random to work the frame on hot tempered Jimbo Ochoa.

That is on the one hand. On the other is the possibility that Castano was killed by Jose Herrera. The proximity of the heated argument to Castano's murder is more than coincidence. But in this case, why put the frame on Jimbo? Again there is a lack of connection. Why point a finger at a man who has no motive? It makes no sense. Santiago has interrogated the hotel staff and no one saw Jimbo leave or enter the hotel between the hours of midnight and eight a.m. This does not actually provide him with an alibi but it also weakens Santiago's case against him.

I consider retaining a local attorney to represent Jimbo but decide to wait. The producer Henry Blanke is on the way and should arrive around three-thirty. Hiring lawyers is not part of my job description despite Phil's incompetence. I'll leave the attorney up to Henry.

I head into the restaurant to grab some lunch. The chef and I have reached an accommodation. It's simple. I need not be bound by the menu. He will fix me anything I want within reason as long as the ingredients are available. I tested him this morning by ordering a bowl of oat flakes with sliced bananas, brown sugar and fresh milk. It was delicious. For lunch I plan to have a fruit salad made with romaine lettuce and mayonnaise and topped with crushed walnuts . I'm about to sit at an empty table when I spot Alejandro Moreno, the reporter from El Sol de Tampico. I grab Cleo, the buxom head waitress, and order my salad and pull up a chair across from Al.

He's poring over his notes as he nurses a cup of tea. He looks up and smiles. I smile back. Al's the guy who thanked me for the press conference. He's a mousy little guy pushing 50 with a bald pate and sparse hair around the edges. I offer to buy him lunch. He declines. His integrity is not for sale, not even for a burrito. We chat for a few minutes, not about the story, but about the Hollywood mystique. Al is one of millions fascinated by the glamour of movie making. I tell him the glitz of Hollywood is like a chinchilla coat on a twenty peso whore. What you see is not what you get. I don't think he believes me. They never do.

Al's already told me he's been working at El Sol for about five years and before that he was a reporter for El Universal, one of Mexico City's major daily papers.

"So, Al, what can you tell me about Violetta Munoz?"

His head snaps up and he almost allows himself a smile. "You go back many years, Senor Bernardi. And why would you possibly be interested in Violetta Munoz?" he asks.

"Academic curiosity," I say.

"I'm not sure I believe that but in any case I know very little."

"A little is okay," I smile warmly.

He shrugs. "Well, I can tell you it was a major story for many weeks. This was maybe a dozen years ago. She was the daughter of Armando Munoz, a man very close to the president. Her body was found in a hotel room, dead of an overdose of heroin. Or at least that was the eventual finding. There were those who believed that she was a victim of foul play because of her association with known members of the criminal population. Despite cries of cover up and corruption, the story eventually died and was forgotten."

"Do you remember the name of the police officer involved in the investigation?"

"No, Senor, I do not. To learn that, you would have to have access to police records." A thought comes to him. "Or you might talk with Federico Nunez."

"Who's that?"

"He covered the story for our paper. A year later he resigned and took a job teaching at UNAM. Sorry, that's Universidad

Nacional Autonoma de Mexico. The city's major university. The last I heard Federico was planning to write a book about the affair but I don't know whether he ever got around to it."

I've scribbled some notes on a little pad which I always keep in my jacket pocket. Moreno's curiosity has been piqued.

"Is there something about this you would care to share with me, Senor?" he asks.

"Not at the moment. Perhaps later."

Before he can follow up with another question, I steer the conversation around to El Jefe. I figure if anybody can give me the real goods on this bastard, it'll be Al who's been around since the days of Pancho Villa.

"So, Al, since I'm new to Tampico. tell me about El Jefe," I say.

He shrugs. "You had your Al Capone, We have our Rodrigo Fuentes. That is the name he was born with. Jefe is the name he lives with. And, Senor, if you please, the name I live with is Alejandro, not Al."

"Sorry. Just trying to be friendly. So, El Jefe, where's he from?" I ask.

Moreno shrugs. "Some say Juarez. Others say Mazatlan. El Jefe does not say. Without seeing his police record I can tell you who he is. A boy brought up on the streets who learned early to lie and steal. A boy without family except for those like him, in or out of prison."

"Yes, I can imagine. What's he into," I ask, "besides extorting the studio to hire half of Tampico to work on the film?"

Moreno smiles. "El Jefe is a man of broad interests. Let me see. We have the brothels, of course. A thriving trade. The lllegal lottery. I believe in the states you call it the numbers racket. Very profitable. Cock fights every Friday and Saturday night. Now and then trucks filled with expensive goods disappear from the roads leading to town. I've been told the drivers are not hurt. They may even get a cut of the proceeds as high as 5%. And then, as you pointed out, there is the extortion. El Jefe does not call it this. He offers the local hotels and cantinas protection from vandalism and other crimes, asking only a modest weekly contribution to his coffers."

I nod appreciatively. "A vivid picture, Alejandro. I take it you don't write about these activities."

"To what purpose, Senor Bernardi? If I did, my newspaper would not print them." I frown at this and he smiles. "Did you know, my friend, that in the past six years we have not had one incident of newspapers undelivered, work stoppage in our press room, or intimidation of our news vendors?"

"I understand."

"For all his faults as a human being, El Jefe is a very astute businessman. He never asks for great amounts and because his demands are modest everyone pays. He gives no trouble and he gets no trouble. While no one is exactly happy, everyone cooperates. Only Chief Santiago seems to take his operation as a personal affront but what can he do? If no one complains, where is the crime?"

"And murder?" I ask.

"What about it?" Moreno asks.

"If there is no threat, then there is no power. How far does he go to keep people in line?"

Moreno nods. "Yes, I see. Well, Senor, certainly not murder. A modest beating now and then. More severe in some cases, but never murder. That is not his way. You remember how it was with your Mr. Capone? Everyone looked the other way when it was just bootlegging but when the killing started, that was the beginning of the end." He regards me curiously. "Are you suggesting El Jefe might be responsible for the death of Senor Castano?"

"It crossed my mind."

Moreno shakes his head. "No. That is not possible."

I drum my fingers impatiently on the table. I am annoyed. First of all, my salad has not arrived and I picture the chef out back plucking bananas from a tree. Secondly, Moreno's assessment bothers me. He could easily be wrong but he seems too sure. I have learned never to dismiss a good newspaperman's instincts and he easily could be right .

"I'd like to meet him," I say.

"El Jefe?"

"Yes. Could you arrange a meeting?"

Moreno laughs. "You do not need me to introduce you, Senor. El Jefe is very approachable."

"Really? And exactly where do I approach him, Alejandro?"

"His office. La peluqueria de caballeros. The barber shop." He points. "It is called Rodrigo's and is on the main street, Monterrey Boulevard where it meets the Avenida Benito Juarez. You will have no trouble finding it."

I'm amused. "And he is a barber in addition to his other talents?"

Moreno shakes his head. "His office is in the back. I presume if you go you will not be carrying a weapon."

"Only a fountain pen," I reply.

Moreno smiles knowingly. "I think perhaps El Jefe does not know how dangerous a weapon that can be."

I nod. I like to think he's right.

I stop at the front desk and ask for a map of the city. It looks like a walk of maybe twenty blocks. It's warm out but not stifling. I decide to hoof it. I need the exercise and the fresh air.

"Joe!"

I turn. John Huston is approaching.

"I just got the word. We resume filming tomorrow morning," he says.

"Good news."

"What the hell's going on with Jaime Ochoa? Are they going to let him out or what?"

"I don't know. I wouldn't count on it."

"Damn," he says in frustration. "I need him, Joe. The other A.D.the Mexicans stuck me with is a basket case. Totally worthless. Worse, his English is dreadful. This is going to cost us another day, minimum."

"I'll talk to the Chief," I say.

"Do that, Joe. I'll put up bail money. Anything."

"Henry Blanke's on his way, John," I say.

"Screw Henry. You're here. He isn't. Just get him out."

"I'll do my best," I tell him. I'm beginning to resent this associate- producer-by-process-of-elimination position I'm in. Henry can't get here fast enough to suit me.

I start walking toward Monterrey Boulevard and I know that as long as Captain Iglesia is on the scene, Jimbo stays where he is. This is a by-the-book cop and Santiago is doing what he's told. Maybe when Henry Blanke arrives, and if he hires a local lawyer, just maybe something can be worked out. If it isn't, Huston is going to make Henry's life miserable.

I wander through the narrow streets taking in the sights and sounds of this thriving coastal city. The pace is leisurely. People smile a lot although they are not well off. Many may be poor but I don't get a sense of poverty. The people I know in the states are driven to succeed, to attain more and more, even though for many of them, their days are lived in fear and uncertainty. Here I feel none of that. I wonder who has the right outlook, these simple people or the ambitious denizens of Los Angeles. The more I see of the rest of the world, the more I realize how insular my life in Hollywood has become.

Monterrey Boulevard is a wide thoroughfare boasting myriad shops and restaurants and office buildings. The street is crowded with cars though most are at least ten to fifteen years old. The boom in new cars coming out of Detroit has yet to hit Mexico. In some ways I think Tampico is at least a decade behind the rest of the world. Soon it may catch up. I wonder if that is a good thing.

I find Rodrigo's barber shop. It is small and non-descript. There are two chairs and both are occupied. The barbers are jabbering with their customers which seems to be a world wide phenomenon. Two men are waiting their turns. Both look up sharply as I enter and look around. One of them stands and approaches me. He is pug-ugly with an acne-scarred complexion and a big black bushy mustache. I notice he doesn't really need a haircut. I also notice he is carrying a pistol the size of a sledgehammer in the holster under his left arm.

"May I help you, Senor?" he says, almost pleasantly.

I look around. Everyone is Hispanic. I am the gringo in a strange land. "I wish to speak to El Jefe," I say.

The man shakes his head. "There is no one here by that name."

I point. "I think in the back of the shop there is a man by that name or perhaps Rodrigo Fuentes. I will speak to either one."

I wait for a smile. I don't get one. The man's English is lousy or he doesn't think I'm funny.

"What is your name, Senor?" he asks.

I tell him. I also tell him I work for the movie company. His eyes perk up when he hears this.

"You will wait," he says. "I will be back momento."

He goes. I shuffle my feet nervously. The conversation between the barbers and their customers has stopped. I have become an object of considerable interest. The older barber is looking me up and down as if measuring me. I remember that in the days of the old West, the barber was often the undertaker and the coffins were custom made. I shuffle my feet a little more anxiously.

The mustache with the gun appears in the rear doorway and waves me forward. He ushers me into a decent sized room which looks like an office as well as a den. There are two pinball machines against the wall and a pool table at the far end. At the other end is a massive desk behind which sits El Jefe. Seated nearby is another man who I take to be his brother Fredo. I can tell by the black eyes, bruises and bandages.

El Jefe beckons me forward.

"Just so you are aware," I tell him emphatically, "people know that I have come here."

He smiles showing perfect teeth which are probably all capped. "Do they? I am so delighted."

"My name is Joe Bernardi----"

"I know who you are. What can I do for you, Mr. Bernardi?"

"I want to talk to you about Pedro Castano."

He frowns as if not recognizing the name. He looks over at his brother who says quietly, "The actor. Muerto."

El Jefe nods and turns back to me. "There is nothing to talk about. I did not know the man."

"Which means, I suppose, that you did not kill him or have him killed."

He laughs and looks back at his brother who also laughs. He shakes his head and looks at me, almost with amusement. "What are you doing here, Mr. Bernardi? Why have you come into my office with your insulting accusation? Why do you dishonor me?" I listen for a trace of anger in his voice but there is none. He is mostly curious.

"Someone killed Mr Castano, moved his body to the rock quarry and then went to a great deal of trouble to direct blame at one of the company's crew members, a man named Jaime Ochoa who is being held at the city jail."

"And how does this concern me?" El Jefe asks.

"Maybe not you, Jefe, but perhaps your brother." I look over at Fredo. "It was Jaime Ochoa who gave your brother those cuts and bruises. Perhaps he felt a need to even the score."

Fredo rises quickly from his chair but El Jefe puts out his hand, halting him.

"I do not have to listen to this," Fredo says angrily.

"Sit down," El Jefe tells him.

Fredo hesitates but then sits. A rage shines from his eyes. Without Jefe in the room to curb him, I could be dog meat.

El Jefe gestures to a chair by the desk.

"Sit down, Mr. Bernardi, and listen to me very carefully," he says. "I will tell you this once and once only."

I sit, still eying Fredo warily.

"I did not kill this actor. My brother did not kill him. He and I are not in the business of murder. I believe that Jesus Christ is my savior and I will not face him with the blood of another man on my hands. I believe Alfredo feels as I do but if there were the remotest possibility that he had killed this man to implicate your friend and I were to find out, I would send him back to the slums of Juarez to live out his days." He turns to his brother. "Is that not so, Alfredo?"

"It is so, Rodrigo," he says quietly.

"I am a businessman, Senor Bernardi. I buy and I sell and I

am well paid for my merchandise and my services. I do not cheat a man unless he cheats me first and the people of Tampico know you only get to cheat El Jefe once."

"Es verdad," Fredo mutters.

"You will find this hard to believe, Senor Bernardi, but I am beloved by the people I do business with. That is right. Beloved. Do you know I am also beloved by the bishop and his priests? Yes, that is true. And you ask, why? How can this be, this man who runs whores and fosters gambling and stages cock fights. I will tell you how it can be. A grocer needs to protect himself against the criminal element and so I agree to provide that service. And for what sort of money do I provide it? The figure is negotiable but always small. A weekly payment of ten pesos, maybe twenty. The equivalent of a basket of tomatoes or a bushel of corn. That is all. No more. Dozens of times in the past years others have tried to push me aside. They feel my people can pay more, much more. But I do not ask it of them because I am content with what I have. But these others, these jackals would extort ten times what I do. They would spread misery and despair everywhere and this I cannot allow so I forcefully discourage them. I give them a lesson they will not quickly forget. And because of this we have peace in Tampico."

I look into his eyes and there is no doubt that he is telling the truth. It is bizarre and yet it makes perfect sense.

"What about the movie company? I've been told that you take half of what your people earn."

"That is a lie. I am given 10%. I am, how do you say it, an agent. 10%. Is that not usual?"

I have to smile. This gangster is doing a good job of emulating the William Morris office. "I was also told that you demanded the company hire ninety men instead of thirty."

He nods. "That is true because I know of ninety men with families to feed who need the work. Does your company pay a high daily wage? It does not but I do not make this an issue. I know how business is done. Money is always available for what you people call "labor peace". Is that the right phrase? Yes, I think it is. You are shooting a scene on the street. A storekeeper disrupts you by operating a chain saw. He is given a few pesos. He puts the chain saw back on the shelf. I know that these things happen all the time, am I not right?"

"Yes. you are," I admit.

"Fine. So I go to Mr. Drago and ask him to put ninety of my people on the payroll. All are capable of hard work and will do as they are told. He tells me he does not need ninety people. I say, maybe not today but maybe tomorrow. Anyway it would be a gesture of good will. He says he will hire thirty and that is all the good will I am going to get. We talk more and then he starts to call me names which involve my parentage. I will not repeat them here. I am immediately aware that the man is no gentleman and also that he is very stupid. I take my leave, promising myself that very shortly he will be begging me to provide those sixty other men. Oh, and did I mention that in addition to being rude and stupid, he is also pigheaded. I am still waiting for his call." He smiles. "Do you have any questions, Senor?" he asks.

"None," I say. "I believe I may have misjudged you, Senor Fuentes."

"El Jefe," he says.

"El Jefe," I say.

"Gracias," he says.

"I will accept for the moment that neither you nor your brother had anything to do with Pedro Castano's death." El Jefe nods. "Do you think it possible, considering your wide ranging contacts throughout the city, that you might develop some information about the person or persons actually responsible?"

Now he smiles. "I find that interesting," he says thoughtfully.

"I am not authorized to speak officially for the company but I would imagine that we could put up a modest reward for such information," I tell him.

"That is even more interesting, Senor Bernardi. I am always in favor of seeing justice done."

"Good," I say, rising from my chair. "I will be in touch."

I turn to go and hear his voice.

"Senor," he says sharply.

I look back and he is coming around the desk toward me.

"In my country," he says, "it is customary when two men strike a bargain that they shake hands."

He puts out his hand.

"In my country as well, Jefe," I say as we shake.

In a few moments I am back out on the street, momentarily blinded by the bright sun. I start to trudge back to the hotel and as I do, I begin to wonder what in hell I have gotten myself into.

CHAPTER TEN

"Reward? What kind of reward?" Henry Blanke demands to know.

"I told him modest," I say.

"Modest? What the hell does that mean?"

"I don't know. Maybe not very big."

My producer looks at me with withering skepticism. We're sitting in the office just vacated by Phil Drago who I have not seen since I walked into the hotel fifty minutes ago. I wonder if he is already on his way to the airport.

"Now let me get this straight," Henry says. "You have offered a reward to El Jefe for his help in finding out who killed Pedro Castano when it may actually be El Jefe who is responsible."

"I don't think so," I say.

"You don't think so," Henry says incredulously. "Did you know that Police Chief Santiago thinks so. Or at least he thinks it is a probability."

"The Chief has his own set of problems with El Jefe. If a rainstorm were to flood the city streets, Santiago would suspect El Jefe of seeding the rain clouds."

Henry smiles. "Well, if your Jefe comes up with something I'll play along but I won't let him put a gun to my head."

"Fair enough," I say. "Now can we talk about who's in charge around here?"

"I am."

"For how long? Are you staying? I mean, I've had just about enough of Phil Drago."

He nods. "I understand. My fault. I thought Phil could handle it. Now I see he's been in way over his head."

"Is he going back to L.A.?"

"Not at the moment. I'm going to keep him around to run errands. If he keeps his eyes and ears open, he might actually learn something."

"You don't mind if I disagree."

"You won't be the only one," Henry says. "Now about these other sixty workers. What do we do?"

"You want my opinion?"

"I believe I just asked for it."

"For what we'd have to pay them, put 'em on the payroll. That'll be the end of the vandalism and cheap at the price."

He nods. "I'll have Burt call this Jefe guy and work it out." Burt Yarrow is our unit production manager. He handles budget and payroll, among other things.

Henry reaches in his shirt pocket and takes out a pack of Herbert Tareytons and his lighter. He flips his Zippo and lights up.

"Have you talked to Martinez lately?" he asks.

"The guy from the film commission?"

He nods. "He's set up a memorial service for Castano at eight o'clock tomorrow morning at the Church of the Immaculate Conception. He hopes for a good turnout. I told him attendance by our people would be compulsory. He was pleased."

"Huston won't be pleased." I say.

"John's okay with it," Henry says. "Look, Joe, the film

commission's under a lot of pressure from the government to do something about this killing and I am going to make sure we do our damndest to look like we care."

" Be nice if we really did care."

"That, too," he says. "Now, the newspapers are going to have a front page spread in their morning editions so we could have a big crowd on hand. Play it up big. Warners is the studio with a heart. Make us look good."

"Done," I say. "And speaking of making us look good, are we getting a lawyer for Jaime Ochoa?"

"Taken care of," Henry says. "His name's Diaz and I'm told he's the best in the city. He doesn't think he can get Ochoa out on bail, they consider him a flight risk, but he'll do the best he can."

"If he gets him out, he'll be a hero to Huston."

"So John told me." Henry sighs and leans back in his chair. He shakes his head wistfully. "Movies are so much fun to watch, Joe. Why do they have to be so damned difficult to make?"

I leave Henry's office and head for my room. I don't get far. The foreign press has arrived en masse and are loaded with questions, most of which I can't answer. They all want to interview Jimbo Ochoa. I tell them it's not going to happen. They want verification of rumors that there has been labor trouble on the set. I say there were a couple of minor incidents. Everything has been cleared up. There will be no further trouble. They want to know if the national police, the federales, has taken over the investigation. I refer them to Captain Iglesia who is registered at the Tampico Majestic Hotel. They've heard that Bogart is squabbling with John Huston. Untrue, I say. They keep it up. They can't take untrue for an answer. I remind them of the memorial service the following morning. I can tell from their faces they won't be attending. Reporters on assignment away from the office generally drink into the wee hours of the morning and sleep in until noon. To be fair, not all. Just ninety percent of them.

By the time I get to the door to my room, I need a shower. Jesus told us to love our fellow man but he never met a nosy reporter from a third rate newspaper. I go inside half expecting to find Bunny there to surprise me. My only surprise is that the bed is made and she is not hiding behind the shower curtain. After I clean up, I give her a call.

"Where are you?" I whine like a jilted schoolboy.

"Can't make it, Joe. Bud's got other plans for me," Bunny says. I can hear the disappointment in her voice.

"What can be better than Bogart, Huston and a juicy murder?"

"Nothing. But tomorrow night I have to join a gaggle of my peers at a press conference for Larry Olivier who's over here drumbeating for his new movie, the tenth or twentieth remake of 'Hamlet'".

"Oh, God. Really? What next from the old hambone? A four hour version of Lear?" I suggest.

"I sure hope not," Bunny says, "though in fairness I hear it's a pretty good movie."

"It had better be," I say. "I doubt America is ready for florid Elizabethan and an effete hero in tights and a codpiece."

The more I hear her voice the lonelier I get. The lonelier I get the angrier I get and when I finally hang up I am pissed at the world in general and at Jose Herrera in particular since he has just risen to the top of my shit list. Without El Jefe to lay Castano's killing on, Herrera is squarely in my sights. I vow to myself to get to the bottom of all this as quickly as possible so I can go home and fall into the arms of the woman I love. Or at the very least, admire greatly.

The Cathedral of the Immaculate Conception is a magnificent 19th century edifice that dominates the Plaza de Armas. Light tan in color, it boasts tall and imposing Corinthian columns and three massive doors that lead into its heart. Valuable paintings and other works of art decorate its walls and its altar has been stunningly carved from Carrera white marble.

The pews are jammed. There is not a seat to be had. As advertised, the local papers dedicated their front pages to the ceremony, both featuring a large flattering photo of Castano. There is a photographer on hand, flitting about and taking pictures of everything in sight. Perhaps tomorrow the papers will have a page one followup.

Bogie and Tim Holt and the two Hustons are seated up front alongside Carlos Martinez. I am told he will deliver the eulogy although I was unaware he even knew the man. Maybe in Mexico that is unimportant. I look for someone up front who might possibly be the widow, Luisa Castano, but I see no one. I scan the throng for Hal Croves and Herrera and finally spot them at the far end of a pew, halfway back. The members of the crew are in evidence as I knew they would be. The press is absent, again as I knew they would be. The pews toward the rear are crowded with townspeople, most of whom are probably here only for a glimpse of Bogart.

There is no casket as the body is still in the hands of the city coroner. The Bishop, a gentle looking man with flowing white hair, conducts the service in Latin. Martinez delivers the eulogy in English. It is flowery and unspecific and as I suspected, he almost certainly did not know the deceased.

At nine fifteen the bishop blesses the crowd with a 'Dominus vobiscum' and we all pour out into the sunlight. The temperature is still bearable and a slight breeze is coming in off the water. I spot Santiago standing under an oak tree in conversation with Captain Iglesia. I stroll over.

"Buenos dias, Senor Bernardi," the Chief says with a smile. Iglesia nods his head in greeting. "A lovely service did you not think?" he says.

"I did," I lie turning then to Iglesia. "Good morning, Captain," I say.

He nods again."Good morning," he says.

"I am curious about the autopsy, Chief. I spoke to the widow by phone. She's pretty anxious to claim her husband's body."

"Of course," Santiago says. "Perhaps they will finish this afternoon. Certainly by tomorrow. I will let you know."

"Gracias," I say. Again I turn to Iglesia. "I'm curious, Captain. How did it go with your interrogation?"

"What interrogation is that?" he asks.

"Jose Herrara. The argument I witnessed between he and the victim the afternoon before he was killed."

"Ah, yes," he says, nodding. "I talked to both Mr. Herrera and his friend Mr. Croves. It is as he said. The two men were together all afternoon. I am afraid you were mistaken, Senor Bernardi."

I'm startled by this. "I'm afraid I am not mistaken, Captain. I have many shortcomings but blindness is not one of them."

"Of course not." Now he is oozing familiarity. "From a distance it is easy to misidentify someone. It happens often."

"The man was Jose Herrera. I will swear to it."

Iglesia shrugs. "And they will swear otherwise. I am a good judge of people, Senor Bernardi. They are not lying."

This guy's as smooth as oil on a baby's butt and I am getting pissed. "You may choose to believe that, Captain. I don't."

"That is your privilege," he says dismissively.

A moment ago I was annoyed. Now I am steamed at this pompous, straight-backed ass of a bureaucrat posing as a policeman.

"Damned right it's my privilege. You turn a blind eye to a legitimate suspect while my buddy cools his heels in your cell---"

"Your buddy?" Iglesia interrupts in amusement. "A man you only met a day or two ago---"

"That's right. My amigo, my friend, my buddyboy. I read people right away, Captain and I'm really good at it. And let me tell you, I have you read right down to your government issue tin badge."

Santiago feels compelled to jump in. "Senor, I do not think this is the time or---"

Iglesia ignores him, boring in on me. "Be careful, Senor Bernardi. You overstep your bounds."

"Not yet I don't, Captain. But after I write my article about the arrogant stupidity displayed by the policia federale as they botch this case, then we can discuss what bounds I've overstepped."

If looks could kill, I'd be dead. Iglesia takes a breath and regains control. "Hear this, Senor. As far as the official police investigation is concerned, Senor Herrera is not involved. I suggest you not waste any more of your valuable time and accept the fact. You will excuse me."

With that he walks off. I watch him go. "Highhanded son of a bitch, isn't he?"

Santiago shrugs. "He is a federale. It comes with the job."

"Your el presidente ought to fire his ass."

"Oh, no, Senor. The federales, they are never fired."

I nod knowingly. "Really? Sounds just like los Estados Unidos." Underneath my pleasant exterior I am fuming. Since I know I didn't misidentify anyone, I am now even more convinced that Herrera is involved. What bothers me is why a captain of the national police seems to be playing along? And even worse, why is Chief Santiago letting him get away with it?

"Tell me something, Chief," I say, "just what do you know about this Captain Iglesia?"

He shrugs. "What is there to know? His credentials are in order. I even telephoned Mexico City to verify them."

"Aha!" I look at him with newfound admiration.

"What is this 'Aha' business, Senor?" he asks.

"Just that you, too, smell a rat."

He shakes his head. "I smell no rat."

"Really?" I say. "Then how come he showed up here by himself?"

"He has two men with him."

"Two men? Wow," I say, unimpressed. "Usually these guys travel in packs like starving jackals. Where are his investigators? His forensic people?"

"Perhaps you should ask him."

"Yeah, perhaps I should. And maybe I should ask him why he hasn't talked to the members of the company. You did. And I wonder why he hasn't scoured the neighborhood for another possible witness to the argument Castano had with Herrera. I wonder if he has been able to come up with a motive for Jimbo to commit murder. Has he even tried? In short, Chief, I'm wondering what the hell this guy is doing here and you should be, too."

Santiago's back stiffens and I realize I have probably gone too far. "I need no advice from you, Senor Bernardi, on how to run my office. Con su permiso," he says as he turns and strides away. I rue my outburst. I truly believe Santiago is a decent dedicated cop. I hope I haven't screwed up our relationship.

I start down the street. I may walk to the hotel or I may hail a cab. I haven't decided. I have a lot of thinking to do. Out of nowhere a man steps in front of me. It's Barbershop Bob, El Jefe's security goon with the mustache under his nose and the cannon under his left armpit.

"You follow me." he grunts and starts off. I'm afraid of cannons. I do as I'm told. He leads me across the street to where the Packard is parked. As I approach, El Jefe steps out of the back along with an older man dressed in white cotton work clothes. Jefe smiles in greetng.

"Buenos dias, Senor Bernardi," he says. I respond in kind. "How do you like my church?" he asks. "Is it not beautiful?" I agree that it is. "The bishop is a very good friend of mine. He allows me to take holy communion every Sunday provided I come to confession every Saturday. He gives me Hail Marys to say. I give him pesos to support the church and the school. We have a good arrangement."

"The bishop is fortunate to have you as a friend, Jefe," I say.

"I told you, Senor, I am a friend to all. This man here by my side. He works for me. He is also my friend. His name is Esteban. This morning he tells me something that I think will interest you. He says that the man you honored this morning, this actor Pedro Castano, at one time he was a police officer in Mexico City."

"Gracias, Jefe, but this is something I already know."

"Es verdad?" Jefe is either impressed or pretends to be. He turns to his friend and they start back and forth in rapid fire Spanish. Whatever they are talking about, Jefe is skeptical and Esteban is certain.

Jefe turns to me. "My friend Esteban says that the newspaper story this morning is not the truth. This actor, this former policeman, is described as an honest and virtuous man. Esteban says this is not so."

I turn to Esteban. "Are you sure about this?"

"I am sorry," El Jefe says. "Esteban speaks no English but he is positive. He says that on two occasions, he personally saw the man he worked for hand envelopes with cash to this detective."

"I find that hard to believe," I say.

"That may be, Senor, but Esteban is a most reliable man and he does not lie. Not to me."

"And this man he worked for? Does he have a name?"

"That is not important," Jefe says.

"But if I wanted to verify-----"

He addresses me as he would an unruly child. "I think it would be most unwise of you to try to do that, Senor. Most unwise."

I nod. "Yes, you're probably right," I say, thinking how stupid I just sounded.

Jefe smiles broadly. "And now, Senor, perhaps we could discuss the matter of my reward."

I shake my head. "That reward would be for help in identifying the killer, not something like this."

"Si, si. Yo comprendo," he says quickly. "But I thought, perhaps a small token, a gesture of good faith, for valuable information."

"Okay. How much?" I ask, unsure how valuable this information might be.

"Oh, no, Senor. I do not wish money. But perhaps if you were to speak to Senor Bogart, an autographed picture with my name would be most appreciated."

He smiles hopefully. I can't believe it. This master criminal is nothing more than a big kid with an autograph book.

CHAPTER ELEVEN

El Jefe offers to drive me back to the hotel but I politely decline. I found yesterday's walk invigorating. I opt to do it again. On the way I stop by police headquarters. I find Santiago in his office and ask if I can see Jimbo Ochoa. He tells me no. Jimbo's with his lawyer. I ask if there's any chance he'll be let out on bail. Santiago shakes his head apologetically. Even if he personally were able to recommend it, the Captain is vigorously opposed. Although he is holding Jimbo's passport, Captain Iglesia is afraid the company will find some way to spirit Jimbo back to the United States and thereby cheat the firing squad. I ask Santiago if somewhere in this process a trial might be involved. Possibly, he tells me, with a shrug. Fed up with Mexican justice and unable to help my friend, I leave.

At the hotel I find Alejandro Moreno, the reporter for El Sol de Tampico, on the veranda, again enjoying a cup of tea. This is a stroke of good luck because, had he not been there, I was going to call him at his newspaper. I pull up a chair beside him.

"Buenos dias, Alejandro," I say.

"Buenos dias," he responds.

"I didn't see you at the memorial service," I say.

"I have been to many. They are all alike."

"That smells slightly of cynicism," I say.

"Realism," he says. "My business is telling the truth."

I nod. "In the interest of truth, I might have a job for you."

"I have a job."

"This would be something on the side. Relatively easy and it won't take long. It would also pay well."

He regards me thoughtfully. "I'm listening," he says.

"I need some research done in your morgue, your old newspaper files which I assume go back quite some time."

"You assume correctly, Senor."

"I would do this research myself but I understand very little Spanish."

"And what sort of research would this be?"

"I need to know everything you have on a man named Bruno Traven and his friend Jose Herrera. Particularly Mr. Herrera."

Moreno frowns. "Mr. Herrera is the man who is here with Mr. Croves."

"That's right."

"And Senor Croves?"

"I'm not interested in Mr. Croves."

"But you are interested in Bruno Traven."

"Yes."

Moreno gives this considerable thought.

"Is there something you wish to tell me, Senor Bernardi?"

"Not now," I say. "Maybe later."

Moreno nods. "And when you say you will pay well?"

"Two weeks salary."

"A month," he says.

I nod. "A month. But I need it quickly."

"In that case, I am wasting my time sitting here." He downs the rest of his tea, gets up and extends his hand. We shake and he leaves. If there is anything of interest in the files of his news-paper, I'm pretty sure Moreno will find it.

The lobby is pretty much deserted. The company is at a cantina several blocks away filming the big fight scene between the stunt doubles. I imagine Huston is happy to be back to work but he will never be able to make up the time he's lost. That means overages and overages mean more wrath coming from Burbank in the form of memos from Jack Warner. The one Huston received yesterday was pretty devastating, dictated by Warner after seeing dailies. Warner pointed out that in one scene, automobiles of the late 30's and early 40's were clearly visible, even though the picture is supposed to take place in 1927. When I asked John about it, he shrugged. If they're paying attention to that sort of thing, he said, we've lost them and everything else will make no difference.

As I head for the stairs, Burt Yarrow, the unit production manager, catches up with me.

"Joe, glad I caught you," he says. He hands me a sheet of paper. "We've recast the part of the Gold Hat bandit. Guy's name is Alfonso Bedoya. It's all in there. Name, credits. I've got photos coming by special delivery." I nod, checking it out. Bedoya has a lot of good credits. "He's going to cost us a lot more than we've budgeted. Man, that guy Castano's quotes were pretty low. Don't know how he made a living. Anyway, it's all yours. Tell the world." Burt walks away and I head for my room. I need to get a press release out right away but first there's an important call I must make and it can't wait.

The voice that answers the phone is female but it isn't Luisa Castano.

"May I speak to Luisa, please," I say.

"Who is this?" the voice asks crisply, bordering on rudeness.

I realize now it's a young voice. Maybe one of the daughters. I tell her who I am. Now I hear muffled conversation. The daughter has covered the mouthpiece. It sounds like an argument and then Luisa Castano comes on the phone.

"Senor Bernardi, buenas tardes."

"Buenos tardes, Senora," I say.

"My apologies. My daughter Angela, she is very protective of me. I have not slept well the past few days. She worries."

"I understand. I had hoped to see you at the memorial service this morning," I tell her.

"I do not travel," she says matter-of-factly. She doesn't elaborate. "Have you news for me? About my husband's body."

"They should be able to turn it over to you tomorrow."

"Thank you. I will make arrangements."

"Senora, I have a question. I have been told that before your husband became an actor, he was a police officer."

"That is correct."

"That's very unusual," I say.

"Yes, I suppose it is."

"May I ask how it came about?"

"Of course," she says. "It was eleven, perhaps twelve years ago. Pedro was working security for a movie company on the streets of Mexico City. An actor failed to show up and they needed someone to play this small part of a revoluntionary. Pedro volunteered and they were very pleased. A month later they were making another film and they asked if he would be interested in a larger role in this new movie. It paid well enough. Better than what he was earning as a police detective. He was happy, like a little boy. For me, I did not like giving up the security of the police job but I said nothing. And then when they had finished filming, he brought home two thousand pesos. A bonus, he said, for signing a contract with the movie company. In those days two thousand pesos was a great deal of money. I felt we were very blessed."

Again, I express my condolences and then I ask."What sort of police officer was your husband, Senora? You said detective. Was that homicide or vice? Just exactly what did he do?"

"He never talked much about his work. I think vice, yes. Prostitutes. Sellers of drugs. Not homicide. I am fairly certain of that."

"Anything political? Anti-government terrorism, perhaps. Anything like that?"

She shakes her head. "No. I am sure not."

"And how long had he been a police officer before he switched careers?"

There is a moment's silence. "He was a year out of the academy when we met. Another year before we married. Angela is nineteen. That would be eight years, perhaps nine."

"Think back. Did he ever mention the name of a man called Jose Herrera?"

"No, I don't think so. That is so long ago and as I said, he did not talk much about his police work. No, I'm sorry. I do not know that name."

"And his work as a detective? Was it all in Mexico City?"

"Yes." Now she sounds troubled. "Senor Bernardi, why do you ask these questions?"

"Just gathering information," I say.

She is smarter than that. "You think perhaps my husband's death is related to his work as a policeman, even after all these years?"

"I don't know, Senora. I just don't know," I tell her.

After I hang up, I think long and hard about the argument I

witnessed between Castano and Herrera. I now have a new perspective. Castano, the police officer, and Herrera, very possibly an anarchist cut from the same cloth as his friend Bruno Traven. Castano recognizes Herrera for who and what he is. There may be warrants out for him. It now occurs to me that Herrera might not even be his real name. Whatever it was there was blood anger between them. I am praying that Alejandro Moreno finds something useful. I wonder now if I shouldn't have asked him to also check out police captain Miguel Iglesia who is either very dense or worse, is directly tied to Herrera. I also wonder if Iglesia was picked for this assignment by his superiors or if he volunteered.

My thoughts are interrupted by a knock on the door. I open it. Carlos Martinez is standing there holding a large manila envelope. He smiles and tries to peer past me curiously.

"Forgive me, Senor Bernardi, I hope I am not intruding," he says.

"You mean do I have a naked chambermaid hiding in the closet?" I ask. "Afraid not. Come on in."

He laughs a little as he moves past me. "I will not take up much of your time." He hands me the envelope. "My photographer took many pictures this morning of the service. There are several of Mr. Bogart and Mr. Huston and other cast members. I hope you will find them useful."

I smile in gratitude. He has reminded me that I probably should have had the release out a couple of hours ago. This business with Jimbo in jail is muddying up my concentration.

"Thanks. I was just about to get on it."

Martinez shrugs. "A nuisance, I know, but a necessary part of the process. At one time I, too, produced motion pictures. Oh, nothing as grand as this. Low budget, what do you call them, quickies?"

I nod. "Quickies."

"Still, you must have a script and a camera and actors and when you are finished, you must tell the world."

"Anything I might have heard of?" I ask.

He laughs. "I don't think so. Peasants fighting the federales. The federales fighting the peasants. The stories didn't change much. I think I am very fortunate the presidente gives me this job on the film commission because I think I was not a very good filmmaker."

"By the way," I say, "this morning you forgot to mention Pedro's career as a police officer before he turned to acting."

His eyes widen. "Police? I had no idea of such a thing. Es verdad?"

"Si."

"To be truthful, I hardly knew the man at all. I suppose that was apparent."

"Forget it. You did well under the circumstances."

"Gracias," he says with a half hearted smile. He tugs at his collar. As usual he's being attacked by the sweats. He looks around nervously. He has something on his mind and can't quite get to it. His eyes fall on my water pitcher on the dresser. "Would you mind, Senor. I have a bad thirst."

"Help yourself," I say.

He pours himself a full tumbler of water and drains it in one gulp. He sighs. "Bueno", he says replacing the glass.

"Anything else, Senor? I am at your disposal," I say by way of helping him get to the point.

"Si. A small thing, Senor Bernardi. I dislike even bringing it up. I hope you will not take offense."

"Try me."

"This situation. The arrest of Mr. Ochoa. The delays in

shooting. I am concerned that if great care is not taken in the presentation of the news that the situation will reflect badly on my people."

"I don't think so. We've received nothing but total cooperation and Chief Santiago has been more than fair."

"Yes, yes," he says nervously, "but I know the low regard in which my countrymen are held by some people in your country. Not all. Not even most. But I hope not to see articles or releases which reflect badly on my country and my people."

"You won't see any coming from me. That is a promise, Senor Martinez," I say.

He reaches for my hand and shakes it vigorously. "Gracias, Senor. I had hoped to hear as much. I will notify el presidente. He will be most grateful."

Continuing to sweat, he goes out. In a way I feel sorry for him. He reminds me of a lot of middle-aged middle level people at the studios. Unable to control or trust those beneath them and scared stiff of those above them, they live every day in fear of their jobs. I pray I never find myself in that position.

I open the envelope and check out the photos. They're good and he's given me about two dozen of each shot. I'll pass them out to the jackals at the six o'clock news conference. Meanwhile I have a press release to write. Requiescat in pacem, Pedro Castano. Vaya con Dios.

CHAPTER TWELVE

Rain is pelting the hotel. It is heavy and wind driven and shows no signs of abating. It started around five o'clock, waking me from a sound sleep as moisture from my open window whipped at me, even as I ducked under my covers to avoid it. I had forced myself to get up and close the window, knowing the air inside my room would soon become stiflng. A sheet of lighting lit up the courtyard below followed by a rumble of thunder only a moment later. The core of the storm is close by. I get back into bed but now I can't sleep. Hard questions and the absence of answers had kept me up well past midnight. Now they have returned.

We are in the heart of Tampico's rainy season and I suppose we should be grateful for the many clear days we have had. I search my brain but can't remember what's scheduled for this morning. I think maybe the outdoor construction site where Bogie and Tim are working for Bart MacLane. If that's the case, we're about to fall another day behind.

I walk into the production office a little past seven thirty. Phil Drago is at a table off in the corner running the mimeograph and collating script changes. He glances over at me but neglects to smile. I'm not sure I blame him. He's been reduced to gofer status for the rest of the shoot. Burt Yarrow tells me the company's back at the cantina filming some pickup shots for the big fight scene they started filming yesterday.

I pick up a memo pad and write a note to Bogie asking for the photo inscribed to El Jefe. I tell him I know it sounds weird but the guy is helping get Jimbo cleared. I'll explain later. I put the memo in Bogie's mail slot, grab a coffee and a banana and order up a car to take me to the set.

When I walk in I see they haven't started shooting yet. Ted McCord, the cameraman, is setting up the lights. I give a little wave to Ken and Moe who wave back. Off in the corner Croves is sitting in a camp chair writing in a yellow lined legal pad. Herrera is a few feet away carefully watching the crew at work like a hawk sizing up his next meal. I wonder if Croves is writing a book along the lines of 'How These Idiots Screwed Up My Book'. Burt Yarrow has told me that Croves and John Huston had gone at it pretty good last night. Croves probably isn't aware that Huston is on his side when it comes to fidelity to his novel. Croves really ought to be screaming at Jack Warner who is the one causing all the trouble through surrogates.

I wander across the room and sidle up to Ken.

"What do you hear about Jimbo?" he asks.

"Same old, same old," I say. "I'm working on it." I lean in closer and put my back to Croves and Herrera. "Do you suppose you might be able to grab a couple of still shots of those characters without their knowing about it."

He glances in their direction. "No problem," he says. "Give me a couple of minutes." He walks away and when he comes back I can see he has a compact 35 mm Argus clutched secretively in his right hand. He winks at me. Just then Henry Blanke walks in and when he sees me, he makes a beeline toward me. His body language suggests I am not about to hear the latest joke from Hollywood. He takes me by the arm and steers me off to the side where we won't be overheard.

"What's going on, Joe?" he asks.

"About what, Henry?"

"You know about what," he says. "I got an earful from the cops this morning."

"You mean Captain Iglesia," I say.

"That's the guy. He says you're interfering with his investigation. He strongly suggested I ship you back to Los Angeles."

"I'm not surprised," I say.

"So what's the story?" Henry says.

Since he's asked I tell him. The argument. The phony alibi supplied by Croves. Iglesia's support of Croves and Herrera and disbelief of me. I also throw in that Iglesia is either stupid or he's on somebody's pad.

"So you take it upon yourself to play junior G-Man which as far as I know is not part of your job description." He shakes his head helplessly. "Joe, what am I going to do with you?"

"If I were you, Henry, I'd start by believing him."

We both turn to look. We hadn't noticed but Bogie's been sitting in his camp chair, noodling with a crossword puzzle, and he's heard everything.

"Look, Bogie---" Henry starts to say.

"No, you look, Henry," Bogie says, getting to his feet. "I think Joe makes a lot of sense. This Captain Iglesia, I didn't like the looks of him first time I laid eyes on him. One of those guys with a puffed up ego. What does Chief Santiago say?"

"Not much," Henry says.

"You mean he kept his trap shut," Bogie says. "Yeah, he would. Santiago's a straight shooter. He'd have backed Iglesia if he'd agreed with him."

"So what do you think I ought to do?"

"Besides giving Joe a raise?" Bogie smiles that crooked smile of his. "Just kidding, Henry. My advice? Do nothing. If Iglesia tries to throw his weight around, call Jack in Los Angeles. That'll start the pot boiling. Yeah, Jack taking on the federales. I'd like to see that." His smile is even broader as he walks away.

Henry turns to me. "Sorry, Joe. You're right. Bogie's right. Ochoa's not going to get railroaded as long as I'm around. Forget we had this conversation."

"Thanks, Henry," I say.

"And if you need to keep digging, do it."

"I will."

Henry claps me on the shoulder. "Let me know if and when you need backup."

He walks away. I look across the room at Croves and Herrera. The boys went crying to the cop. The cop went crying to my boss. And now? And now I am more convinced than ever I am on the right track. All I need now is a little corroboration from Al Moreno. I glance over toward Ken. He grins and gives me the high sign. Mission accomplished.

I walk over to the bar and try to communicate with the owner of the cantina who seems to be fascinated by all the activity. My Spanish is lousy and his English is non-existent but after a few minutes I am able to get him to place a call to El Sol of Tampico. I'm connected with the news desk but told that Alejandro is not in and no one has seen him. Message? No, no message, I say. I'll call back later.

For want of something better to do I stick around for the filming. Croves is still doodling on his yellow pad and Herrera is still watching silently. Several times I catch Herrera looking in my direction. He looks away guiltily. An hour into the shoot he goes to Croves, whispers in his ear, and then walks out. By noon he still hasn't returned.

The rain has stopped and I'm told that after lunch the company is going to move to the construction site which is about mile away toward the gulf. I decide to skip it. At twelve-thirty Huston wraps the set. The caterer has set up lunch on the sidewalk outside. Plank tables, dozens of chairs and a menu of Mexican staples. This I will pass on. I talk the owner into making another try at the newspaper office but the story is the same. There has been no sign of Alejandro Moreno.

I get a weird feeling. Not that I'm worried but something doesn't feel right. Call it a reporter's instinct. I had it overseas during the war. I still have it. I decide to check out the newspaper office for myself. I confer with the cantina owner. He points, gestures left, then right and holds up five fingers. I am hoping he means five blocks and not five miles.

The air is cool and crisp and still smells of the storm that has just passed through. I walk briskly, avoiding the many puddles on street and sidewalk. The rain has continued to hold off even though dark clouds are threatening to unload at any moment. I pick up the pace since I am wearing my best suit and I have no umbrella. As I turn a corner I see I am almost there. I jog to the entrance and duck inside. The rain continues to hold off.

I climb the stairs to the second floor where the directory says I will find the newsroom. It is bigger than I thought it would be but at the moment, it is pretty much deserted. El Sol's a morning paper. Things will start to get hectic around late afternoon.

A pretty young girl is sitting at a desk near the doorway. I take her to be a secretary, maybe a proofreader. I ask about Alejandro Moreno and get the same story. He hasn't been in. No one has seen him. I ask which desk is his. She points it out. I start toward it. She doesn't try to stop me so I keep going. I think it possible though probably not likely that Al has done some work and it's in his desk. What the hell, it's worth a peek. I try the middle drawer. Locked. So are the others. Nice try, Joe.

"Senor Bernardi!"

I look up and Moreno is striding toward me and though I have always considered him a harmless, mousy kind of guy, he looks furious.

"What do you think you are doing?"

I shrug. "I was hoping to rifle through your desk drawers, but I see you keep them locked up. A wise move, Al. Keeps out nosy interlopers."

His eyes narrow. "I do not appreciate your humor, Senor."

"Most people don't," I say. "I tried to reach you several times this morning. I was hoping you'd have some information for me."

"I have no information, Senor Bernardi," he says. "In fact I am no longer interested in your proposition."

"Was it something I said?"

"Please leave, Senor."

"Look, Al, we had a deal----"

"And my name is not Al. Now do you leave or do I call security?"

"What happened, Al? Cold feet or did someone buy you off? How about if we pay you two months salary? Three?"

Moreno reaches for the phone. I raise my hands defensively. "Okay, okay. I get it. I'm leaving. Sorry I bothered you. I knew that a lot of the cops in this country are bought and paid for. I just didn't know the graft extended to the press. I won't make that mistake again."

I turn on my heel and stride toward the stairway. Now I'm the one who's angry and I'm starting to wonder who I can trust. The more I see of Mexico, the less I like it.

Downstairs, I huddle in the alcove by the front entrance. The rain has resumed and it is steady and heavy. Across the way I see a sign, Parada de Taxis, and couple of waiting cabs. I debate whether to wait it out or make a dash for the cab stand and possibly ruin my suit. Having never been a patient man, I grab a newspaper from a nearby stack, hold it over my head, and race out the door. Immediately I think this is a bad idea. I step off the curb into the gutter and my feet are ankle deep in raging waters. I plow ahead. Just then a car comes by, nearly hitting me, and skids to a halt. It sprays dirty street water all over my trousers. I turn to scream something obscene as two men leap from the car. They are big and burly and quick and in an instant, they have my arms pinned back and my jacket coat pulled up over my head. I struggle to no avail. I cry out but I'm sure no one hears me as I feel myself being dragged. I am tossed into the back of the car with two men pressing my face down onto the floor. A heavy foot pins me there as the car speeds away.

CHAPTER THIRTEEN

We have been driving for at least twenty minutes. I am still pressed against the floorboard of the car with a heavy foot on my neck continuing to keep me immobile. There are three of them. The two who grabbed me and the man behind the wheel. They are jabbering in Spanish but I have no idea what they are saying. I can hear the rain drumming on the car roof and the metronomic rhythm of the windshield wipers. The sounds of traffic, so heavy when we started, have now almost disappeared. I'm sure we are heading into the countryside. I have tried to listen for clues as to our route. Road conditions, bridges, railroad crosssings, factory whistles. I fail miserably. It all seemed so easy in those dime novel paperback mysteries. Only in bad fiction does this sort of thing have a chance of succeeding.

The car turns, veering off pavement onto loose gravel. I am aware of tree branches swiping at the car and I realize we are driving deep into a forested area. The sounds of gravel cease. We start to slip and slide. Our road has turned to mud. I have been gripped by fear ever since I was grabbed. Now it is worse and I pray that my bladder will not embarrass me. I don't want to give these pigs the satisfaction. My foster mother always said to wear clean underwear. You never know when you will be in an accident. I wonder how she would feel about urine soaked skivvies. The rutted road which is jouncing my kidneys into pulp is not helping matters.

Finally, the car comes to a stop. Sharp orders are given in Spanish. I hear the rear door open. Someone grabs me by the collar of my jacket and drags me out of the car. I am pushed forward and stumble to the ground which is wet and slimy. The men laugh. I turn and look at them, All three are dark, swarthy Hispanics with Indian features. One of them pops open the trunk and takes out a spade. He walks over to me and head nods me to get up. I feign ignorance. He leans down and grabs my shirt collar and pulls me to my feet. He holds out the spade. I look at it dumbly. He shakes it at me. I back up a step and shake my head. He steps toward me and pulls a pistol from a shoulder holster. He aims it between my eyes and holds up the spade. Hesitantly I take it. He backs up a couple of steps and points to the muddy ground. I know what he wants. I tell myself I won't do it but when he points the gun again, I start to dig.

We are in a clearing. Trees soaked with rain water surround us on every side.The rain has abated to a soft drizzle and the ground is wet and soft . It will not be hard work and it won't take long. The men are a few feet away by the car, smoking and joking. I'm positive they don't speak English but I try anyway.

"People will be looking for me," I say. They pretend they did not hear me. I speak louder, trying a little Spanish.

"Usteds. El Jefe. Mi amigo," I say.

The three of them look at me. One looks at me, feigning fear. "Ah, si, El Jefe. El bandido grande. Me estoy asustando." All three break into laughter. It wasn't the reaction I had hoped for. I try to think of something else to say but El Jefe was my hole card. I have nothing left in my bag of tricks and nothing left to do but dig.

It isn't long before they break out a large jug of wine and pass it around. Soon they wlll not only be dangerous, they will be drunk. I try to calculate my chances of racing into the forest and hiding and decide they are not good. The guy with the gun has stuck it in his belt and I surmise he could draw and fire in two seconds, probably less. And yet if I continue digging, I am a dead man. I might be able to get close enough to wield the spade but then what about the two other guys? Are they packing? I can't tell.

I'm down less than two feet into the muddy hole when the gun guy calls out to me.

"Senor! Basta!"

I know enough Spanish to know that 'basta' means 'enough'. I look at him curiously. He signals me to climb out of the partially dug grave. This is not good. The wolves will be getting at me in less than a day. I climb gingerly out of the muddy hole carrying the spade. With his gun he waves at the spade indicating I should toss it away. I do so. He slips his gun in its holster and moves to me, sticking his face only inches from mine. He smells of cheap wine and stale cigarettes and his expression is one of undisguised malevolence.

"Now you listen to me, Senor," he says.

My God, he speaks English. I start to open my mouth.

"No, you listen. I speak. I can kill you now. This is my choice but I think maybe I will not do so. Not yet. You are a man who asks too many questions about things that do not concern you. The unfortunate death of the actor is none of your business. Your stupid attempts to help free your friend, your buddyboy, are misguided and dangerous. You are to stop. You are to stop now. Do you understand me?"

"Yes," I manage to say.

"Do I have to repeat what I just told you?"

"No."

He looks deep into my eyes. "Then, for now, you live." With that he grabs my shirt collar with his left hand and throws a vicious right hand into my solar plexus. I gasp and my brain lights up like a pinball machine. Roughly he shoves me backwards and I land in several inches of water that have collected in the shallow grave. I cannot breathe. I cannot open my eyes. I hear more laughter and then the car engine turns over. It backs away and drives off. I am alone and hurt and wet and it is very, very quiet.

I am soaked through to my skin and I thank God this is Tampico and not Nome, Alaska in the dead of winter. I try to piece together what has happened. I haven't been killed and except for one punch, I haven't been beaten. Something the gunsel said is eating at me and I'm trying to figure out what it was.

I struggle to my feet and start to climb out. I slip on the slime and fall back in. On the third try I manage to get out. I have no idea where I am or how far I have traveled from Tampico. I start down the dirt road, water sloshing in my shoes. I am dripping mud from head to toe. The tall trees and the overhanging branches have created a canopy which has shut out all light. I shuffle forward laboriously taking baby steps a few inches at a time. My left foot hits the side of a rut and my ankle twists. I almost go down as the pain shoots up my leg. It's not a sprain but it hurts like hell and I find myself going even slower.

To my right I hear a noise in the underbrush. Something alive is moving about and chances are its eyesight is better than mine. Ignoring the pain I pick up the pace. Close by I hear the screech of a bird followed by the howl of a wolf. That noise in the underbrush, it seems to be paralleling me. Suddenly I stub my toe. I reach down and my hand wraps around a large rock. I clasp it tightly and pray I won't need to use it.

At that moment, the muddy road turns to gravel and I know I am getting close to a paved road. I try to go faster, limping badly, but my body rebels. My belly hurts but I'm pretty sure my ribs are intact. The fear is starting to leave me to be replaced by anger. It is a cold and calculating anger because it has come to me. The thing that was bothering me. I now realize who sent these goons to terrorize me.

I stagger and stumble on the gravel surface for what seems like an eternity but is probably less than ten minutes. Up ahead I see the occasional car speed by, some with lights on. Night is starting to fall. When I reach the paved road, I am gripped by indecision. I can't remember which way we turned onto the gravel. Do I start to walk left or right? If I guess wrong I could end up in some god forsaken wildnerness inhabited by snakes, iguanas and jaguars, none of whom will be glad to see me. I need help badly and I need it now.

A car is approaching from my right. I ignore my pain wracked leg and run into the middle of the road, waving frantically. I am framed in his headljghts. He must see me. Maybe he does but he has no intention of stopping or even slowing. I dive to my right onto the shoulder as the car whizzes by me. I struggle to my feet to flag down a car coming the other way. He blares his horn at me and makes an impolite gesture. I am ready to panic when I hear a chug-a-chug-a-chug-a and very old Model T flat bed truck approaches from behind me. I wave again as he drives past and just when I think he is going to continue on, he pulls to the side of the road. I race to catch up.

The driver is a wizened old man with a frail frame and a wrinkled face beneath thick white hair. He smiles and if he has any teeth I can't see them.

"Muchas gracias," I say.

"De nada," he replies.

"Do you speak English?" I ask.

He shrugs blankly.

"Habla usted anglais?"

He shakes his head.

"Tampico," I say.

He nods and points in the direction he is traveling. Then he gestures for me to get in the car. I do so gladly. He starts up again and we chug-a-chug-a-chug-a along the road, passed by everything on four tires but I don't care and neither does the old man. He has an old portable radio next to him on the seat and he turns it on. It starts to blast lively Mexican music into the cab. He laughs and throws me a wide grin as he starts to beat time on the steering wheel. I join him on the dashboard. Neither of us is Gene Krupa but we are having a hell of time.

Within an hour we are driving down Monterrey Boulevard in Tampico. I spot Rodrigo's barber shop and now I know where I am. I point to a nearby corner.

"Aqui," I say.

"Si?" he asks.

"Si," I reply.

He comes to a stop at the corner. I reach into my wallet and take out a 10 peso bill. I try to give it to him. He shakes his head and waves it away. I become more insistent. His expression turns dark. "No, gracias," he says firmly. I nod and put the bill away. I reach out my hand.

"Muchas gracias, amigo", I say.

He takes my hand with a smile. "Con mucho gusto, amigo," he says as we shake.

I get out and watch him drive away. I am immediately ashamed of all the crappy feelings I was beginning to have about the Mexican people. Life is not total shit after all.

CHAPTER FOURTEEN

I am lathered with soap as hot water cascades onto my head and then swirls downward over every pore of my body. My joints are no longer aching as they once were and although my belly has a gorgeous purple bruise to remind me of my ordeal, I am once again feeling like a member of the human race. I am pretty sure I looked like no such thing when I walked into the hotel lobby less than an hour ago. Henry was the first to spot me but I fended off his questions. I'll explain later, I told him. Several of the crew members stared at me curiously as I labored up the stairs to the second floor.

I towel off and look over at the bed. A huge piece of me wants flop down for a good night's sleep but I resist the temptation. I have business to conduct and it won't wait. I've called a bellman to come for what's left of my suit. I tell him it probably can't be saved but to have the cleaners conjure up a miracle. In the meantime I slip into a blazer and slacks and an open collared shirt. If this outfit gets destroyed I'll be wandering around bare-assed the rest of my time in Tampico.

I step out of my room to see a familiar figure leaning up against the wall waiting for me.

"You clean up well, old top," Phineas says. "Care to tell me what mudhole you've been wallowing in and why?"

"Definitely not," I say.

"Most assuredly it has something to do with the case," he ventures.

"Possibly," I say. "How'd you do with that lead I gave you?"

"Quite well, thank you, Joseph. My research skills were in top form. Castano's first role was as a peasant freedom fighter in a movie called 'Vamonos con Pancho Villa" made in 1936 starring Domingo Soler. I couldn't get much out of the Mexican police even though I talked to a few old timers who remembered back that far. What do they call it? The 'blue wall of silence'? In any event, cop to actor. That's a fine human interest story in my humble opinion."

"Since when has your opinion ever been humble, Phineas?"

"Seldom, I grant you. Now what next, old top? What have you got for me?"

"Nothing," I say.

"Fine. Then I'll just make something up and dare you to deny it," he says petulantly.

"Sounds like a real career builder," I say.

As we start down the stairway to the first floor I'm startled by a sudden outburst of hooting and hollering and then applause coming from the lobby. When we reach the bottom step I see that a couple of dozen crew members are crowded around Jimbo Ochoa who is grinning from ear to ear. Next to him, also smiling, is an older Hispanic gentleman who I take to be his lawyer, Luis Diaz. Henry emerges from the bar to see what the ruckus is and he, too, starts to smile. I don't know quite what's going on but it has to be good.

At that moment Jimbo spots me and waves. He knifes his way through the crowd to get to my side and throws his arms around me in a great bear hug.

"Hey, Joe. Thanks, man. I don't know how you did it but wow, this feels good."

I'm puzzled. "I don't think I really did anything, Jimbo," I say.

"Well, I hear you've been on their ass for the past three days. That's good enough for me."

"So what happened?" I ask. "Did they drop the charges?"

He shakes his head. "They let me out on my own recognizance. The studio's taking responsibility. If they can clear this murder thing before the company goes back to the States, no problem. If not I might have to stay but my lawyer thinks they've got a zero case against me."

"Any news about the baby?" I ask.

"Santiago let me make a call. Katey's fine for now. I'd sure like to be with her but fat chance I have of getting out of Mexico."

I look at Phineas who has been jammed up against my elbow, drinking it all in. "There's your story, old top," I say. "Go write it."

I look past Jimbo and see that Chief Santiago has entered the hotel. He exchanges a word with Diaz and then the two of them walk over to Henry. They talk for a moment and then all three walk into the bar. I clap Jimbo on the shoulder, say something encouraging that I don't believe and leave him to Phineas who is already steering him away from the other reporters.

They're sitting at a table in the far corner. Henry looks up as I approach.

"Joe, are you okay?" he asks.

"I'll live," I say.

Henry turns to the others. "Joe walked in about an hour ago, soaking wet and covered with mud."

"Well, that happens when somebody grabs you and takes you for a ride into the countryside," I say. I look down at Santiago. "Jimbo's release. Where did that come from? Your idea?"

"No, I was told," Santiago says.

"By who? Iglesia?" My tone is testy and I don't care who knows it.

Henry shakes his head at me. "Joe, back off."

"Sorry, Henry, it's a little late for that."

"Ochoa's release was arranged at the highest level," Henry says.

"I guess that means Jack Warner threatened to pull the entire shoot out of Mexico if the kid wasn't set loose. Yeah, that would make sense. Mucho American greenbacks are involved here."

"Joe, I'm serious. Let this alone," Henry warns me sharply, no longer smiling.

"Well, you know, Henry, I'd like to but a few hours ago I was grabbed off the street, driven to God knows where and forced to dig my own grave at gunpoint. This is all getting very personal and I am getting very pissed."

Diaz, who I don't know, pipes up. "And who could blame you, Senor? I think you were lucky to escape."

"I didn't escape. I was let go. The whole thing was a big scare tactic." I look back at Santiago. "Where's your pal Iglesia?"

"At this moment, I don't know," he says.

"It'd be nice if you could find out. He and I need to talk."

Henry points to an empty chair. "Joe, why don't you sit down," he says.

"No, thanks. There's a kid out there in the lobby who thinks he's off the hook for the murder charge, who thinks he's gotten a fair shake from the Mexican authorities but we all know better, don't we, gentlemen? I think I've seen enough of Mexican justice and police tactics to last a lifetime. I don't know what Iglesia's game is but it's rotten and it's self serving and if you think I was a pain in the ass before, well, as Jolson would say, you ain't seen nothin' yet."

I turn on my heel and start out. Henry calls after me. I ignore him. If there's a pink slip in my message box in the morning, so be it. Warners isn't the only studio in Hollywood. I go out the front door and down the steps and stop in the parking circle to stare up at the sky. The moon is nearly full and the inky darkness surrounding it is peppered with silvery pinpoints everywhere I look. The rain is gone. There are no clouds. God is in his Heaven but sadly, he's not paying a lot of attention to what's going on in Tampico.

A familiar odor invades my nostrils. The dung heap. I turn. Santiago is behind me puffing on his noxious little cheroot. He looks at me sadly. "This has been a difficult day for you, Senor. I am truly sorry."

"Thanks," I say curtly.

"Please believe me when I say I knew nothing of what happened to you," he says.

"Maybe not. But your friend Iglesia sure does."

"He is not my friend," Santiago says. "I do not know him. I do not wish to know him. I work with him because I must."

"All right," I say flatly, conceding nothing.

"You might be mistaken," he says.

"I'm not."

I know I'm not because one of the goons described Jimbo Ochoa as my buddyboy, a phrase I used just hours before in my set-to with Captain Iglesia. It is an American phrase. No Mexican uses it offhandedly. Iglesia's goons screwed up royally and Iglesia's going to pay the price.

"I marvel at your certainty, Senor Bernardi. It is even possible you are right. I will try not to betray my feelings when I have breakfast with the Captain tomorrow morning in the dining room of the Tampico Majestic Hotel." He stares at me hard and then shakes his head ruefully. "My mistake. I should not have divulged this eight-thirty meeting to you. A thousand apologies. Buenos noches."

He moves past me toward the sidewalk where I see he has parked his cruiser. He gets to the car door, relights his cheroot, then gets in and drives off without a backward glance. I smile. Eight-thirty at the Tampico Majestic. When I get to my hotel room, I set my alarm clock for seven-forty-five.

At eight-fifteen the next morning, I grab a cab and head for the heart of the city. On the way I stop by the barber shop. El Jefe's not there but I drop off the glossy of Bogie who has not only signed it but inscribed it, "To my amigo, El Jefe". This should net me a bagful of gold stars.

The Tampico Majestic Hotel is located near the Plaza de Libertad. It is six stories high with a stucco exterior and a tile roof. The main entrance is utilitarian and there is nothing to suggest that this is the hotel of choice for the city's more affluent visitors. But when I enter, everything changes. The lobby is huge with velvet wallpaper and walnut trim. The carpet is lush and the pile is deep. Sofas and easy chairs abound for the comfort of its guests. Off to the right I can see a hallway which seems to feature myriad shops including women's wear, jewelry, a beauty salon, a men's barber shop, a camera store and possibly a book outlet. To my left is the entrance to the dining room. It is 8:45. I have given Iglesia and Santiago a chance to get settled before I barge in uninvited. I step inside the open archway and even though the room is crowded, I spot them immediately sitting at a small table by a window that looks out over a colorful garden.

As I approach, I spot another table nearby where the goon with the gun and one of his cohorts is sitting. They spot me. A look of panic crosses the gun guy's face and he looks quickly toward Iglesia who doesn't see him. He doesn't know what to do but by then it's too late because I am at Iglesia's table and hovering over him like a vulture drooling over his next meal.

"Buenos dias, Captain," I smile, then nodding to Santiago. "What a pleasant surprise," I say. "I come in for breakfast and here you are. I have been very anxious to talk to you." I grab an empty chair from a nearby table and sit down, the smile never leaving my face.

Iglesia looks at me coldly. "I do not wish to be rude, Senor, but Chief Santiago and I are discussing police business."

"Oh, don't mind me. I'm fascinated by police business. And that reminds me, would this be a good time for me to report an attempted kidnapping?" I look from Iglesia to Santiago and back to Iglesia, a hopeful look on my face.

Iglesia squirms. "I am sorry, Senor---"

I override him by leaning forward very close to him. Half-covering my face, I say, "The reason I ask, Captain, is that two of the men who tried to abduct me are sitting only a few feet away from us. No, no, don't look. Don't let them know I've spotted them." I frown." Well, wait a second. I'll take another look, just to make sure it's them."

I make a production of looking and then I turn back to Iglesia. "You know, I may be wrong. They don't look like kidnappers. They look more like, uh--- police officers. What do you think?"

I shoot a quick glance at Santiago who is sitting stonlly. I think he is trying to suppress a laugh.

"If you are trying to be funny, Senor, I fail to see the humor," Iglesia says.

"Funny? Not me. Captain. I feel anything but funny. A man has been murdered leaving behind a widow and two daughters. No laughs there. Maybe there's something funny about those two gorillas over there sticking a gun between my eyes and threatening to kill me. No, I can't chuckle over that either."

Iglesia is enraged. I'm speaking softly. No one can hear us.

"So what happened, Captain? That slimy little toad Alejandro Moreno comes to you and tells you what I'm up to and you hire these two baboons to scare the crap out of me. No, maybe I have that wrong. Maybe they carry badges, just like you. Is that how it went down, Captain?"

Peripherally, I catch Santiago picking up a breakfast roll and slowly and deliberately slathering it with butter. I can tell he is enjoying this.

Iglesia is not. He is furious and he is on the brink of causing a scene. If he wants one, I'll oblige. He tosses a sidelong glance toward his two lackeys. Out of the corner of my eye I see the gun guy rise from his chair.

"Oh, good. I've been dying to get a piece of your pet baboon. Thanks for making it easy. I may not be able to beat this jerk but I'm gonna throw the first punch and we'll see how it plays out from there."

He looks into my eyes and he believes me. He raises a hand and waves the gun guy back to his seat.

"What is it you want, Senor?" Iglesia says.

"A couple of days ago it would have been a few straight answers but it's a little late for that now. Just for the hell of it, Captain, I'm going to fly to Mexico City to confer with the American embassy and I'm going to talk them into getting me an audience with your presidente and then I am going unload this truckload of manure onto his desk and see what happens. Hell, he may be as crooked as you are. Maybe not . But it's sure going to be fun finding out."

With that I turn and stride out of the room, having made a

point that even Iglesia cannot ignore. I move through the lobby and am almost to the entrance when a rough hand grabs my arm. I turn to face gun guy.

"Get your hands off me," I say.

"Wait here," he says.

"Not likely, pal," I say, shrugging him off, just as I see Iglesia approaching swiftly. Iglesia nods his boy to take a hike.

"Let's take a walk in the garden," he says.

"I'm allergic to ragweed," I say.

"If you want answers, I will give them to you."

He stares me down, waiting for my reaction. I give it some thought, then capitulate. What the hell, I've chewed on this guy enough for one day.

We stroll past a stand of gorgeous yellow roses and a gardener spraying bug killer as Iglesia leads me to a far corner of the garden where we can talk without being overheard.

"Jose Herrera did not kill Senor Castano," he says.

"I've heard that tune before," I say.

"Jose Herrera is not even his real name, Senor Bernardi. He is one of mine."

"Come again?"

"He is a police officer. He works for me."

"Is that right? And how long has this been going on?"

"Nearly four years. I assigned him ---No, that is not right. He volunteered to go undercover, to befriend the writer Bruno Traven, and to keep me informed of Traven's activities. He has succeeded admirably. Traven is a man who does not open up to strangers. For whatever reason, he has come to like Jose's company. He trusts him implicitly. "

"And he's fed you information about Traven's anti-government activities?"

"Yes, a great deal and helped save many lives."

"Then Croves is Traven," I say.

"Of course."

"And so to protect your undercover agent, you send the goon squad out to scare the crap out of me, is that right?"

Iglesia squirms. "I considered it necessary, yes."

I nod. "What do they call you back in the capitol? Senor Law and Order?"

He frowns. "I do not understand what you say."

"Yeah, I'll bet you don't," I mutter. "So, if I have this straight you're sure that Herrera didn't kill Castano because----?"

I let the question hang between us.

"He is a police officer," Iglesia reminds me indignantly.

"So what? So was Pedro Castano," I say. "What was the fight about?"

He shrugs. "I really couldn't say."

"Oh, come on, Captain, don't crap out on me now, just when weve been doing so well."

He hesitates. "Perhaps eleven or twelve years ago, Jose was working undercover for me. He'd wormed his way into a drug gang that was shipping narcotics into the United States. Castano worked for the Ministry of Security, the metropolitan police. They had a run in. Castano roughed up Jose in front of a couple of the gang members. Even managed to break his nose. Of course, Jose could say nothing without compromising his assignment. Shortly afterwards, Jose was transfered to Guadalajara. The two men never saw each other again until the other day. Castano naturally assumed that Jose was still a criminal and Jose could not break his cover to tell him the truth. That is the whole of it."

I nod thoughtfully. "So let me understand this," I say. "Your man Herrera gets beaten up by Castano, his nose is broken and he is humiliated in front of his fellow gang members. Castano still believes him to be a criminal. He may have even threatened him. And you don't think that possibly this might be a motive for murder?"

"You are insulting, Senor," Iglesia says coldly.

I nod. "One of my better traits. I drag it out when the bullshit starts to creep up over my ankles."

"I have told you---"

"You have told me what Herrera told you, but the fact is, that story may be just a story. It was over a decade ago. Who knows what might have transpired between these two men at that time. Or maybe since. Think about it, Captain. Maybe Castano knew a lot more about Herrera's activities than even you did. Maybe your boy wasn't the saint with a badge that you thought he was."

"Now who is shoveling out the gilipollez, Senor?"

"Hey, Herrera may be innocent. Maybe not. But I am going to Mexico City to find out. And by the way, if you send your bully boys after me again, that will pretty much settle that I am right and you are involved in this whitewash right up to the fancy knot in your Countess Mara tie. Adios, Captain."

I turn and walk away leaving him to smell the roses which continue to be sprayed by the gardener with some foul-smelling brand of pesticide. When I look back, the man is no longer spraying but is watching me depart with a great deal of interest.

CHAPTER FIFTEEN

y noon, the hotel lobby is like a speakeasy ten seconds after the first shrill police whistle has cut through the smoke-filled air. With Jimbo Ochoa freed, the story of the decade has evaporated into a cloud of fairy dust and the press is scurrying to make plane reservations for Brownsville and points north. I am not sorry to see them go. With no diapers to change, I am going to be free to make good on my ill thought out promise to Captain Iglesia. Did I really say I was going to solve the murder of Pedro Castano? Me? I think I've been hanging around Bogie too long.

I check at the desk for messages. There is one. It's from Chief Santiago. It says,'Call me'. I do.

"The coroner's done with his autopsy," Santiago says. "I talked to the widow. She's making arrangements."

"Good," I say. "Do you know when they're shipping the body?"

"I believe this afternoon.":

"Thanks for letting me know, Chief."

"Senor, there is something perhaps you should know. It may be important. Perhaps not. Senor Castano was a very sick man."

That's news. "In what way, Chief?"

"His heart. There was much evidence of deterioration. The

coroner tells me the man would not have lived much longer. A year at the most."

"That explains his reluctance to be examined by the studio doctor," I say.

"As I said, it may be of significance, but who can tell?" Santiago responds.

"Well, thanks for telling me, Chief."

I've made the call from the production office and now as I hang up, I hear my name being called. I look toward the doorway as Carlos Martinez bustles toward me, his face contorted with concern.

"Senor, I heard about your unfortunate experience yesterday. How can I apologize? I do not know how or why this thing happened but I must beg your forgiveness on behalf of my people."

I tell him it's unnecessary. The last thing I need right now is Martinez sweating all over me. He won't be deterred. He shakes his head.

"No, no, these things should never happen. Have you reported this to the authorities? Were you able to see their faces? No, I tell you, Senor, this must not be swept away. We must find the men responsible and deal with them harshly."

"I appreciate your concern, Senor Martinez---"

"Concern? This is not concern, sir," he says, eyes bulging. "This is anger. You are a guest in my country. You are MY guest. These men spit on me and on my Presidente."

I try to convince him that nothing can be done but only because what must be done, I am going to do on my own and I want him and his Presidente out of it.

At last he calms down a little and his anger morphs into continued apology. The transition is so fast and so slick that I wonder which emotion, if either, was genuine.

"We are a good people," he says, taking out a handkerchief and wiping away some of his ever-present perspiration. "We are honest and hardworking and I pray that these animals who terrorized you are brought to justice. I ask only that when you write of these events, please remember that the Mexican people are peaceful and law abiding. For this I will be most grateful." He damn near bows as he backs off and then hurries from the room. Poor Carlos. He tries so hard to sound as if he really cares for "the people" but he just doesn't have the skill to pull it off. I don't fault him for it. It is a common failing among bureaucrats.

I sit down ands pick up the phone again. It takes me ten minutes but I finally get through to Luisa Castano. I offer to accompany her husband's body to Mexico City.

"That is very kind of you, Senor Bernardi, but arrangements have already been made," she says.

"I know but it's the least I can do for you, Senora. I am coming to Mexico City anyway. I would also like an opportunity to meet and talk with you in person, if you feel up to it, of course."

There is a pause and then she says, "Yes, I think that would be a good idea, Senor. I look forward to it."

She gives me the name of the Tampico funeral parlor which is handling the shipment of her husband's body, the number of the Mexicana flight and the name of the funeral parlor in Mexico City which will be handling the final arrangements. As soon as I hang up, I book a seat on the flight. I buy a lightweight carry-on bag at the hotel gift shop and get Castano's home address from the files. I tell Henry what I'm doing. He knows I'm up to much more than a quick overnight to accompany Castano's remains but he doesn't try to stop me. He reaches in a drawer and pulls a few hundred pesos out of the petty cash drawer and stuffs them into my blazer pocket. I thank him and head out. I may be back tomorrow. I'm half afraid if things do not go well, I may not be back at all.

The flight is less than half full. I sit by a window and stare down at the lush Mexican landscape. It is a beautiful country, green with rolling hills and fertile farmland and an abundance of people to work the land and raise crops. I know that Mexico is also rich with minerals and has many areas with vast oil deposits and I ask myself, how can a nation with all this going for it be so poor? It is a nation with a rich heritage dating back to the conquistadores and it is there, I think, that the trouble started. For centuries the peons of Mexico have been subjugated, if not by Cortez, then by the interloper Maximillian and even by their so-called saviors like Juarez and Villa and Porfirio Diaz. So much poverty, so little education. If the Jews are the Chosen people, then these are the Forgotten people.

It is close to six o'clock when we land. The hearse is waiting on the tarmac for the coffin to be unloaded. I introduce myself to Renaldo Sanchez, the undertaker. He is properly solemn and so am I. His English is passable and we chat about the weather. He doesn't ask for details about Pedro's death because he has probably read all about it in the Mexico City dailies. He does, however, ask me what Humphrey Bogart is really like.

The trip to the funeral home is uneventful and as the driver is backing the hearse up to the rear entrance, I see a beautiful raven haired young woman waiting in the open doorway. As I approach her, she smiles.

"Senor Bernardi, welcome. I'm Angela Castano." She puts out her hand. We shake.

Beautiful is an inadequate word. She's not tall. Five four at the most with sky blue eyes and creamy skin that dares you to find a blemish. She's wearing white cotton slacks that fit like a Detroit paint job and a forest green cashmere sweater that advertises every curve in her torso. I force myself not to gape.

"My mother has already given Senor Sanchez instructions over the phone so we can leave whenever you are ready. We are eating at seven-thirty."

I shake my head. "No, no. That is very kind----"

"The matter is already settled. And you will be staying with us. It is no imposition. We have plenty of room."

"Angela, many thanks, but I really can't."

"It will be most impolite of you, Senor, to refuse our hospitality."

She fixes me with an I-dare-you look and I cave. I throw up my hands. "In that case---" I leave the rest unsaid.

Out front, parked at curbside, is a new Mercury Town Sedan which I had looked at only a week ago in L.A. and decided I couldn't afford. I hop in, tossing my bag into the back seat. I try to disguise my envy as we take off into traffic.

As we creep along the crowded streets, I discover that Angela is as bright as she is beautiful. She is in her second year at the University and she is studying civil engineering. She lives at home out of choice and helps her mother care for her eleven year old sister Consuela. Twice I bring up the subject of her father and she artfully ducks to a different subject. In her manner, in the way she speaks, I am pretty sure she was a loving and devoted daughter and I think she is afraid that if she starts to speak of him, she will break down.

We have driven through a commercial area and then a section of shanties and shacks. The road starts to rise towards the hills and the houses become larger and better cared for. I look behind me, out the rear window, and see the city below jammed into a bowl-like valley. I feel the car turn and then abruptly stop and as I look forward through the windshield I see that we are in the driveway of an imposing two story home set back on a large tract of land.

"Bienvenudo," Angela smiles as she hops out of the car. I follow.The house is more than imposing, it is breathtaking. The lawn is a lush green and the garden is in full bloom sporting every color on the pallet. She opens the front door and calls out to her mother as I step inside behind her. We enter a spacious living room, furnished well but not lavishly. Two sofas face each other across from a large wood burning fireplace. The ceiling is high and supports a huge chandelier that boasts more than a dozen light bulbs. Works of art adorn the walls. Several windows let in light which is now fading as the sun begins to settle behind the mountains to the west. I walk to the south facing window and stare out at the panorama below. As I do, the chandelier is illuminated, flooding the room with light. I turn back into the room.

Luisa Castano is by the wall switch. She is sitting in a wooden wheelchair and a colorful blanket covers her legs. I know now why she does not travel. She is an attractive woman with a full round face and a body which was probably at one time extremely alluring but has now grown heavier with inactivity. Her smile helps the chandelier light up the room as she wheels herself toward me.

"Senor Bernardi, I am delighted to meet you at last," she says, putting out her hand. Instead of shaking it, I kiss her fingertips.

"And I you, dear lady," I say.

From her expression I can see I have made the right move.

"Senor Bernardi has agreed to stay with us, Mama," Angela says.

I shrug. "I could not turn down such a courteous invitation."

"Bueno," she says. "I think perhaps you would like to freshen up before dinner. Angela will show you to your room. We will eat in about a half hour. I hope you like enchiladas."

I force my broadest smile. "My favorite," I say.

My guest room is small but neat with a comfortable bed. The bathroom is right across the hallway and before the half hour is up, I have showered and shaved and changed into a fresh outfit I had bought at the hotel's men's store.

At dinner I meet Consuela, the fourteen year old, who is not a beauty but has sturdy good looks that take after her father. She, too, like her sister, is sharp and she seems to have a wicked sense of humor to compensate for her plain features. The meal starts with gazpacho soup followed by the enchiladas and I am delightfully surprised by both. Halfway through I am wondering if it would be impolite to ask for seconds.

The conversation avoids Pedro's murder. Although I do not ask, Luisa volunteers that she is bound to her wheelchair by a freak auto accident nearly twelve years ago. A drunk driver fell asleep at the wheel and crossed into oncoming traffic. Luisa was in the wrong place at the wrong time. I nod. This is perhaps an explanation for something that has been bothering me ever since we pulled into the driveway. Burt Yarrow had told me that Castano's acting quotes were very low meaning he was not well paid. If such were the case, how could he afford this house and the expense of caring for a crippled wife and raising two daughters, one of which was attending University? It made no sense.

"I imagine there was a substantial insurance settlement," I suggest.

Luisa shakes her head. "No, there was no insurance. The man had no license and no job. He went to prison for sixteen months but that gave us little comfort. In those days Pedro was still working for the police and we had very little money. Those were difficult days, Senor, but we managed. And then Pedro got the part in the movie and then a second one and then after that, everything was all right. He was well paid for his work, much, much better than the police force."

I nod, pretending I understand, but of course, I don't. If Pedro wasn't earning much from his career, then where was all the money coming from? The obvious answer leaps to mind and I immediately think back to the shouting match at the gas station between Pedro and Jose Herrera.

After dinner we move to the living room for coffee. Consuela goes off to her room to do homework but within minutes I hear the sounds of latin music coming from upstairs and I suspect the homework has been set aside. Angela stays. I realize she is almost never far from her mother's side.

I tell them both why I am in Mexico City. I am determined to find out who killed Pedro. I describe my kidnapping as well as the deceitful attitude of the policia federale. I am sure the truth about Pedro's death lies somewhere in this city. I take out the photos of Croves and Herrera that Ken took on the set at the cantina and show them to Luisa. She studies them carefully and shakes her head. She recognizes neither man. Angela also examines the photos. She, too, has never seen either one.

"Perhaps tomorrow," Luisa says hesitantly.

"Tomorrow what?" I ask.

"There will be a vigil at the funeral home from noon until ten at night. The notice has already been placed in the newspapers. I think that one or two of Pedro's fellow officers from his days on the force will stop by. Yes, I am sure we will see Pablo, at the very least."

"Pablo?"

"Pablo Rivera. He was my husband's commanding officer and has always been a close friend to the family. He has come to the house twice already to volunteer his services. Yes, I think he may prove to be helpful to you."

"I look forward to meeting him," I say.

I reach out and take her hand in mine. She nods with a smile and wheels herself down the hallway toward her ground floor bedroom. Angela goes with her. The more I see of them, the more I like and admire them both and I don't want to see them hurt. But I know deep down that it may come to that. I know I won't be responsible but I could be the spark that lights the tinder. I walk over to the window and stare down at the city. I am stalling for time because I need to speak to Angela alone and I may not get a better chance.

She beats me to it. "It's a beautiful night, Senor." I turn at the sound of her voice. "I'm going to have a beer on the patio. Would you like to join me?"

She's smiling but she's not flirting. Something's on her mind.

"Why not?" I say.

The patio's out back and I settle into a comfortable rattan chair. Angela follows me out a few moments later carrying two cold beers. I take one and swallow deeply. It tastes good and I can feel myself starting to relax. The moon is high and bright over the western mountains and the air is balmy. Angela sits in the chair opposite me. I regard her thoughtfully.

"Your father's death must have come as quite a shock to you," I say.

"His murder, yes. His death, no. My father was a very sick man."

"Oh?" I say feigning ignorance. "In what way?"

"I don't know," she says. "Over the past year he had lost some weight. He was no longer robust. He had trouble climbing stairs. He became forgetful. There were many signs."

"Did you talk to him about it?"

She smiles. "You did not talk of such things with my father.

I know that he applied for some insurance and that they turned him down. When I tried to find out why, they told me it was confidential."

"Did your mother know?"

"My mother knows only what she wants to know," Angela says.

"I see."

"Did you like my father, Senor?" she asks.

"Yes, the little I knew of him," I say.

"But you are not sure about him."

I cock my head curiously. "Why do you say that?"

"It is obvious. You say you want to find his killer. Yes, I believe that but I think you also have many unanswered questions about who and what my father was."

"You are an observant young lady, Angela." I say.

"My father was a good man, Senor, but he was not perfect. And like you, I have always harbored questions. Things I saw that made no sense. Evasive answers when I asked pointed questions. For the sake of my mother I did not press the issues. To her my father was saintly. I did nothing to disillusion her."

"Not only observant, but kind and thoughtful. You are quite a young lady, Angela Castano." I raise my bottle to her and drink.

"If there is something I can do, some way that I can help you, you need only ask, Senor," she says.

I think about that for a moment. "There is but it might mean learning things you'd rather not know."

"I believe it is better that I do," she says flatly.

I know she means it and whatever her age, I know that this is no child.

"Do you know a professor at the university named Federico Nunez?" I ask.

"Si. I attended his class on writing last semester," she replies.

"Do you think you could arrange for me to meet with him, the sooner the better?" I ask.

"That is no problem. Professor Nunez is in his office every morning at eight o'clock making himself available to his students."

"And tomorrow morning?"

"He will be there."

"Will you take me?"

"I will."

"Are you curious why I want to see him?"

"When it is time for me to know, you will tell me," she says.

We sit in silence for a few minutes more and finish our beers.

The University has no campus. It is housed in a dozen or more separate buildings scattered throughout downtown Mexico City. The Liberal Arts College is located several blocks from the capitol building in what was once an armory. Professor Nunez's office is on the third floor. Angela introduces me and then goes into the hallway and sits on a bench, leaving us alone and our conversation confidential.

Nunez looks nothing like a college professor. He is no older than 40, has broad masculine features and the body of a rugby player. He is wearing a grey sweatshirt, black cotton trousers, and sneakers. I suspect when we finish, he'll be going somewhere to work out. We exchange pleasantries and then get down to business.

"What can you tell me about Violetta Munoz?" I ask.

He smiles. "Ah, Senor, are you planning to make a movie of it? You should. It would be a good one."

"No, just curious," I say.

"I love that word 'just'. It says so little and implies so much.

You have gone to a great deal of trouble to meet with me, Senor, to satisfy 'just' curiosity."

"Did you ever write the book?" I ask.

Now he laughs. "You know about that, too. This is getting very interesting." He sighs. "Alas, Senor, I did not write the book. I did not have enough solid information, only rumor and speculation and printing half-truths is not a profitable way for a writer to spend his life."

He gets up and goes to a bookshelf where he takes down a three ring binder jammed with material. He hands it to me and I open it up. Up front are pages of news stories about the woman's death. It's all in Spanish but I get the idea. The headlines are lurid and the photos provocative. Based upon her high school graduation photo, Violetta alive was a gorgeous young woman with streaked hair, probably blonde and henna. She had a heart shaped face and bee stung lips and though I've learned she was 21 at fhe time of her death, she looked more like 16. The photos of her corpse do her no justice. Although I'd like to pore through all this material I don't have the time so I get right to the point.

"Tell me about Pedro Castano," I say.

He regards me curiously. "You are a friend of the family?" he asks.

"I've recently met them. I like them all."

"Angela in particular?"

"Angela yes, but not in particular," I say.

"And why do you wish to know about Pedro Castano?"

"Because I am trying to find out why he was killed and who killed him and my reasons are very, very personal."

Munoz hesitates. "Whatever I can tell you, and it is not a great deal, will not be comforting."

"I don't care about that," I say, "and neither does Angela. We're looking for the truth."

"I can't help you with the truth, Senor, because I do not know it. Here is what I do know. Pedro Castano was the lead detective in the investigation. At first, his work was diligent. After a week or so, it became perfunctory. When I pressed him for information, he was evasive. At times even hostile. At one point I believe he threatened me to back away from the story or there would be consequences. He was subtle. There was nothing you could point to but it was there."

"Why the change?" I ask.

Munoz shrugs. "I assume he was bought off."

"Even though he had a spotless reputation as a police officer," I say.

"Even though," Munoz replies.

"It was rumored that Violetta died elsewhere and her body was taken to the hotel to mislead the police."

"That is correct, Senor. My personal investigation corroborates that but I cannot tell you where she died. No one knows."

"And was it an accidental overdose of heroin or something else?"

"I truly do not know. If it was murder, there was no shortage of suspects. She dallied with a rough crowd but there was no forensic evidence that pointed to murder. As I told you, rumor and speculation, that was all I had."

"But you are pretty sure Pedro Castano was bought off by person or persons unknown."

He nods. "That is my belief."

I stare down at the file folder in my lap. All this information and I'm still no closer to the truth.

"You will pass this information on to Angela?" he asks.

"I don't know. Maybe not. I don't know what good it would do."

"My thoughts, precisely," Munoz says.

By noon we have returned to the house, picked up Luisa and are back at the funeral home. We've been ushered into a modest sized room where dozens of folding chairs have been set up. The open casket is on a bier against the wall, flanked on both sides by flowers of every description.The sweet smell of gardenias pervades the air. Renaldo Sanchez, the mortician, has done an admirable job of humanizing Pedro's dead features and I can tell that Luisa is pleased. Father Ignacio, her parish priest, is scheduled to drop by at six o'clock to say the rosary. In the meantime, Luisa and Angela will meet and greet well wishers.

The room never becomes crowded but there is a steady stream of sympathizers, many of them good friends of the family. I am introduced to all of them. At my request she does not tell them I am working on the movie filming in Tampico. How many times can I tell people what Humphrey Bogart is really like? Besides friends, others who vaguely knew Pedro from his film work filter in for a quick look. By two o'clock I am tired of sitting and I decide to walk outside for some fresh air. I stretch and look across the street at a pre-war black Buick Roadmaster and I realize it has been parked at curbside ever since we arrived at the funeral home. The man behind the wheel is wearing a Panama hat and he is staring at me intently. I look again and take a step forward. The man ducks his head down, starts the car and pulls away from the curb. This is a man I have never seen before and I hope I never see again because he is not just a tourist taking in the sights.

It is three o'clock when the white-haired man enters. He is probably nearing sixty, a robust six footer with tanned masculine features. His eyes dart everywhere and he misses nothing. He moves with a cat-like grace and even without a badge or a uniform, you know he's a cop.

He squats down beside Luisa and takes her hand in his and speaks to her softly. She nods and I can see her eyes are starting to brim with tears. She looks in my direction and he follows her look. Our eyes meet. She speaks to him quietly but urgently and in a few moments he rises and approaches me.

He puts out his hand and I take it.

"Pablo Rivera," he says.

I give him my name and we shake.

"Some years ago I was a Captain in the metropolitan police. Pedro was one of my trusted officers," he says.

"Yes, Senora Castano has told me about you, Captain."

"Did you know Pedro well, Senor?"

"I'm sorry to say I didn't," I tell him. "We met on my second day in Tampico. We talked pleasantly for a long time. We never got a second chance."

"He was a good man, regardless of what some people might say," Rivera says.

I'm puzzled. "Was there some problem?"

He shakes his head. "No. None. But many people are suspicious of police officers in my country. Even the day before I retired after thirty years of service, people were not sure of me." He shrugs. "It is part of the job."

"Then you never had any doubt of his honesty?"

"None," he says. "And I tell you, Senor, the work he was involved with, the temptations were there."

"He worked vice."

"Si. Drugs, women, gambling. All of that but none of it rubbed off on him. I would have known." He shakes his head. "So many of our people succumbed, mostly in little ways. What the Ministry could pay, it was not enough. At first I tried to fix blame. After a while I gave up and pretended not to see the small instances of graft. But Pedro, no, I do not think he was touched by it. He did his job well."

I nod and then I reach in my pocket.

"Captain, I am going to show you two photos. Tell me if you recognize either one of these men."

I hand him the photo of Hal Croves. He studies it for a few seconds, then shakes his head and hands it back. I hand him the photo of Jose Herrera. It takes only a second. His expression has turned cold as he looks into my eyes.

"Guillermo Santos," he says.

CHAPTER SIXTEEN

Rivera has brought me to the main headquarters of the Ministry of Public Security, known as the SSP. This is the police force which oversees Mexico City in a variety of jurisdictions. Rivera tells me that Pedro Castano was an officer in the SSP's Alfa Group whose chief responsibility is to fight drug trafficking and related crimes. The SSP is totally separate from the Federal District Police to which Captain Iglesia belongs.

Retired or not, it is obvious the moment we walk through the door that Pablo Rivera is liked and respected by his peers. There are smiles and enthusiastic greetings all around, all in Spanish, but I get the gist. We take the elevator to the basement where years of records are kept in boxes which are stacked endlessly on floor to ceiling racks. A half dozen men are busy sorting and cataloging or running to retrieve needed information. Voices are muffled. Considering the amount of activity it is extremely quiet. Rivera buttonholes an elderly gentleman sitting at a desk near the elevator. They banter for a few moments and then Rivera hands him a sheet of paper. The man nods and signals to one of his men who takes the paper, examines it momentarily, and then hurries off down a long aisle to the left. Within minutes he returns carrying a large cardboard box.

We are ushered into a small nearby room which contains a table, a lamp and four chairs. It is otherwise bare. Rivera gestures for me to sit while he opens the box and starts to sift through the material. I notice that the side of the box is stenciled "Diablos Rojos". Rivera tells me this is the name of the drug gang of which Herrera, or Guillermo Santos, was a member.

While I sit silently, Rivera continues to look through the material. He pulls out one or two sheets of paper. After about ten minutes, he leans back in his chair and faces me.

"It is as I thought," he says, "but I wanted to be positive. The man you know as Jose Herrera was a member of the Diablos Rojos, the Red Devils. Not the leader but a high up lieutenant. This was a major drug organization with ties to the United States and Cuba. Pedro was a key member of the Alfa Group task force dedicated to bringing them down. During a routine arrest, words passed between them. Apparently Santos made some comment about Luisa. Pedro ordered his men to keep their weapons trained on the other gang members while he savagely beat Santos within an inch of his life. Santos ended up in the hospital for several weeks. The records show his spleen was ruptured and had to be removed. His left arm still carries pins where it twice had to be reset ."

"And after he was released from the hospital?" I ask.

"Officers were sent to arrest him but when they arrived he was gone. After that there was no trace of him."

I nod. "Aside from the severity of the beating, this is pretty much what I was told by Captain Iglesia of the policia federale."

"It may well be, Senor, that Santos was working undercover for the federales. The entire gang was arrested and imprisoned and the evidence was substantial. The type of evidence that would be supplied by an insider."

"My question is, was that beating sufficient motive for murder twelve years later?"

Rivera shrugs. "Who is to say, Senor? Some men carry hate for a lifetime, some can forgive in an hour. I cannot speak for Guillermo Santos. But knowing Pedro and his devotion to Luisa, I cannot blame him for what he did."

"Yes, I know that you are an old friend of the family."

"Si, es verdad. Luisa's father, Cesar Montoya, was my commanding officer for many years. A fine man. Honest and dedicated. Because of him, Pedro joined the force and I will tell you, he had a bright future ahead of him before he threw it away for this career in acting."

"I'm sure he felt he had good reason," I say.

"Oh, yes, and I suppose he did well enough. But what of now, Senor? What will become of Luisa and the girls? With the police there is the death benefit and the pension. I think there is none of that with the acting."

"You're probably right."

"I will talk to Luisa again. There must be some way I can help. Come," he says, getting up from his chair, "we must go back to the funeral parlor so as not to miss the rosary."

When we step outside, I realize the air has cooled and it feels good. Rivera has parked in a restricted zone at the main entrance but no one has bothered his funny little car which obviously they all recognize. On the way over I had asked him what it was and he proudly described it as a 1936 Renault Vivasix which he keeps in perfect working order. It is a car very cheap to run and maintain, he boasts. Perfect for a retired Captain's pocketbook. Perhaps, but not perfect for a six foot frame, I think, as I squeeze myself into the passenger seat.

As we return to the funeral parlor, Rivera talks incessantly about

Luisa. He is very worried for her and the daughters and how they will survive now that Pedro is gone. I get the idea that his concern goes deeper than mere friendship and that he may have designs on Luisa, despite the twenty or so years difference in their ages. I wonder if she is aware of his feelings and decide she probably is.

Father Ignacio makes his appearance shortly before six o'clock, taking time to comfort Luisa and the daughters and then solemnly greeting many of his parishioners. He is a husky man, broad through the shoulders, with jet black hair and heavily Indian features. In a dark alley, without his collar, he might be considered frightening but here in this room, there is a gentleness about him and a kindness in his eyes. The room is crowded when he makes his way to the front of the room and stands before the coffin, bowing his head. I take this opportunity to duck out into the foyer. I don't wish to be rude but if I thought about God, which I seldom do, it would not be one invented by mankind. I have no brief with those who are comforted by religion. I just don't happen to be one of them.

I return just as the good father is winding down. He announces that internment of Pedro's remains will be held in the churchyard of Our Lady of Guadalupe Cathedral at four o'clock tomorrow afternoon. Again, he speaks in comforting tones as he kneels down next to Luisa's wheelchair. She kisses his hand and then he does something strange. He reaches inside his cassock and takes out a small white envelope which he presses into her hands. He leans in close and whispers to her. She nods and puts the envelope into her purse. In a moment well wishers are lining up to convey their sympathies and I hover in the background. I look over at Angela and again she is looking at Pablo Rivera. I have been observing her all day and though it may be my imagination, when she looks at Pablo Rivera, I do not see much warmth in her gaze.

It is nearly eleven o'clock when we return to the house and

it has been a long day for us all. Consuela is not with us. She's opted to stay over at the home of a classmate and because it is Friday night, Luisa has given permission. We say our good nights and head for our respective bedrooms. I lay back on the pillow trying to sort out what I have learned this day but my brain decides to disconnect and I fall into a deep sleep. When I awake the sun is streaming in my window. My wrist watch on the night table reads 8:38.

I head downstairs looking forward to breakfast when I hear voices coming from the living room. Luisa and Angela are having a heated argument in Spanish and I have no idea what it's about. I think it best to stay out of it so I wander into the kitchen in search of coffee. The percolator is on the stove and it is hot to the touch but before I can pour myself a cup of joe, Angela comes in.

"Senor, my mother wishes to speak with you in the living room," she says. From Angela's tone I sense that Luisa may not be doing so willingly.

She is sitting by the front window staring out over the city. In her hand is the envelope the priest gave her the night before. I approach her.

"Senora?"

She smiles up at me and gestures me to the chair beside her. Angela sits on the window seat, watching her mother carefully."Sit, please, Senor Bernardi," Luisa says. She looks down at the letter that was in the envelope I see, too, that she is holding a key. For a moment she says nothing.

"Mama," Angela prompts her.

Luisa looks at her and then nods.

"Last evening I was handed this letter," she says. "It was given to Father Ignacio by Pedro many years ago. He was to hold it in secret and give it to me only in the case of my husband's death." She stops and looks out the window, unable or unwilling to go on.

Angela reaches over and takes the letter from her mother's hands. "It is in Spanish, Senor. I will tell you what it says in English", she says. "My dearest wife, I am no longer with you. It is a sad thing. Our life together was good and I would have not had it any other way, my precious one. But now life goes on and you must be strong for yourself and for our daughters. In this envelope you will find a key to a safe deposit box in the Bank of Mexico branch office on Alvarado Street. We opened it ten years ago Your signature is on the account. I want you to go---" Angela falters for a moment. "I want you to go with your father to the bank and open the box. What you will find inside needs no explanation. This is important. Go with your father. Do not go alone and trust no one. God willing, I am in Heaven and waiting for you. Do not hurry. I will be patient----" Angela looks at me. "And then he signs it."

Angela puts the letter back in her mothers hands. "My grandfather is dead," she says. "He died two years ago of cancer and now my mother doesn't know what to do. I have told her that she must trust you, Senor Bernardi."

"That's very flattering---," I start to say.

She shakes her head. "It is not flattery. My father would not have written to "trust no one" lightly. Because you are a stranger to us, you are the only one we can trust."

Luisa reaches over and takes my hand. "Please, Senor. I do not know what this is about but I would take it as a great favor if you would accompany me to the bank."

I look into her eyes, almost pleading. I glance at Angela who nods. I look back.

"I am at your service, Senora," I say.

CHAPTER SEVENTEEN

It is Saturday, market day, and the streets are crowded throughout the city and perhaps even more so on busy downtown Alvarado Street. There is no curbside parking spot so Angela pulls into a commercial lot next door to the bank. We pay for three hours but we will be long gone by then. We have brought Luisa's small fold-up wheelchair which she uses when leaving the house. I retrieve it from the trunk and she settles in. It is not comfortable but she makes do.

As we proceed to the front entrance, I glance across the street at the oncoming traffic and spot a black Buick Roadmaster as it creeps by. The driver divides his attention between me and the road in front of him and then he is gone. I have no doubt it's the same car and the same man that I spotted outside the funeral parlor the day before. I say nothing to Luisa or Angela but I am uneasy.

Inside the bank, Luisa is greeted effusively by the manager, a portly little man, mostly bald, with a bushy white mustache and goatee. His sympathy runs deep. Pedro Castano was not only a valued customer, he was a deeply loved friend as well. The world is a poorer place for his passing. God will care for him as he would a saint. He goes on like this for another minute before we get down to business. The signature card is produced and

Luisa signs. She presents the key and she and I are led into the vault area. Only two persons are allowed in at the same time so Angela remains in the lobby.

It is a large box, one of the largest sizes available, and when we pull it out, it is heavy. The manager escorts us to a small cubicle where we will have privacy and then he takes his leave.

I look at Luisa. She nods. I open the box. I half expected it but I am still startled. It is filled almost to the top with bundles of 10, 20, and 50 peso notes. Sitting, she cannot see into the box. I describe the contents and she catches her breath. A look of disbelief crosses her face. All this money? Where did it come from? She is genuinely puzzled. I haven't the heart to tell her that her beloved husband was in all likelihood a blackmailer and furthermore, that it is almost certainly the reason he was killed. No, I will leave that onerous responsibility to someone else.

There is something else in the box. It is a package wrapped in brown kraft paper. It measures about 8" x 8" and about four inches deep. Printed on the paper are the words: "Cesar...You will know what to do with this."

I take it from the box and hand it to Luisa. She looks at it curiously, noting the message. "My father," she says. I nod in understanding.

"What is it?" she asks.

"I don't know, Senora, but I believe it holds the key to your husband's death."

"He meant this for my father," she says.

"Yes, because your father was an honorable man and would do the right thing. But your father is dead and Pedro had not planned on that. Senora, you cannot leave this in the box. It is not only dangerous, it would not be your husband's wish."

"Yes, I see that," she says.

"Senora---Luisa," I say, "do you trust me? Do you trust me enough to take this package and do the right thing with it? To do what your father would have done had he lived?"

She takes another look at the package and then she hands it to me. "Do as you think best," she says. "What do I do about the money?"

"It's yours," I say. "I suggest you spend it."

"And where did it come from, all this money?" She's on edge She really doesn't want to hear the answer.

"I don't know," I say, in all honesty.

I reach in and take out four bundles of bills and hand them to her. "Put these in your purse. They will last quite a while. When you run out, come back for more."

She stares at the bundles in her lap and shakes her head. "I am not sure---"

"Be sure, Senora," I say. "Regardless of how he acquired it, your husband died for this money. Take it."

"He was a good man, Senor. I swear this to you on the life of my children."

I say nothing bcause there is nothing to say and then she slips the money into her purse. Tears are now welling up in her eyes. The woman who was so strong can no longer fight the reality that has changed her life forever. As she starts to weep openly, I kneel beside her and hold her in my arms. Many minutes pass before she can regain control of herself.

We return to the house and I tell Luisa and Angela that I must leave. I apologize for missing the burial that afternoon but I believe I have found what I came for and I must return to Tampico immediately. Luisa understands. She reaches in her purse and hands me the package. I go upstairs to pack my overnight bag. Angela has offered to drive me to the airport. We are not pressed for time. The last flight out to Tampico doesn't leave for another two hours.

Once in my room, I tear the paper from the package. It is a metal box and when I lift the lid, I see that inside is a reel of film. I pull down a few feet to examine it but it is a negative and impossible to read, even with a strong light which I do not have. I replace the film in the box and put the box in my overnight bag. I have not brought much and packing takes no time at all. As I prepare to leave the room, I hear the front door chime and as I reach the head of the stairs, I see Pablo Rivera standing by the front door being held open by Angela. He comes in, fumbles a kiss at Angela's cheek which she manages to evade and then waves to me in greeting as I come down the stairs.

"Hola!" he says with a smile. "Good to see you, Senor."

I wave back.

Luisa wheels toward him. "Buenos dias, Pablo. You are just in time to see Senor Bernardi off. He must return toTampico this afternoon."

He frowns. "Oh, but this is too bad. I have come with excellent news. Come, come," he says moving into the living room. Angela and I exchange a look and then follow him in. He smiles effusively. "My dear cherished Luisa, you know that it has been many years since Pedro was a valued member of the Ministry. And yes, he willingly gave up that calling for a career in the movies. I myself would never have made such a choice.There is great honor in serving one's city and its people. However, he did what he needed to do and that is that." He looks around, smiling smugly. "But before that, Pedro was an exemplary officer with a dozen years of dedicated service and so, I took it upon myself to go to the Director of the Ministry and plead for equity for a grieving widow and his children. Yes, it is true, I say to him, that

Pedro Castano resigned voluntarily but he left behind a legacy of honesty and hard work. Do you not think, I say, that these years should be rewarded with a modest pension, not one that is required by law, but one that is given gratefully from the heart?"

He kneels by Luisa's chair. "And what do you think the man says? He says yes, this man's contribution must not be forgotten and so, dear one, each month you will be receiving a modest check from the Ministry for as long as you live." He beams, waiting for accolades.

Luisa reaches out and takes his hand. "Pablo, only you would think of such a thing. Only you would make this effort on my behalf. I am most grateful."

He shrugs and rises. "It is nothing. A token. But Luisa, my heart is heavy. I worry for you. You will need to live and there is no money coming in. Have you searched Pedro's papers for a bank account or an investment account you know nothing about? Perhaps there is a safe deposit box in some bank."

She looks over at me and I subtly shake my head. She looks back at Rivera. "No, there is nothing like that," she says.

He looks distressed. "I cannot believe it. This is so unlike Pedro, to have left you unprovided for."

"I guess he hadn't planned on dying so young," Angela says with an edge.

"Angela!" Luisa says sharply.

"No, no," Rivera says smoothly. "She is right. It was too sudden. He was too young." His smile returns. "Come, come, let us celebrate the pension. A glass of wine for each of us and then another to honor Pedro, may his soul reside in God's bosom."

"Senor Bernardi and I must get to the airport," Angela says.

"Nonesense," Rivera replies. "There is plenty of time. I insist."

"Yes, it will be good," Luisa says as she wheels herself out of the living room toward the kitchen.

"Angela, help your mother," Rivera says.

She hesitates and then follows Luisa into the kitchen.

Rivera watches her go and then he turns to me. The sympathetic softness in his eyes has been replaced by flint. He steps toward me and he speaks quietly.

"And now, Senor, you will tell me what you were doing at the bank this morning."

"Don't know what you're talking about," I say.

"On the windshield of the car, held in place by the windshield wiper, is a parking receipt for the lot next to the bank on Alvarado Street."

"Is that right?"

"Yes, Senor, it is very right. Now I tell you, and you must believe me, that in my pocket is a pistol and I am prepared to use it. Now I will have what Pedro had kept hidden in that bank."

"Look, I don't know what---"

He flares angrily. "Do not toy with me, Senor. I am perfectly capable of killing you here and now and killing Luisa and Angela as well. It will be messy and I prefer not to do it that way, but I have no fear of being caught. I have many friends in the police. My word has never been questioned."

His look is frigid and I know he means it. "All right, but not here. I want to be far from this house."

"Very well. I will volunteer to drive you to the airport. You will accept. Understood?"

"Yes."

At that moment Angela emerges from the kitchen carrying a tray with a bottle of newly opened wine and four glasses. Luisa is right behind her. Rivera turns to them, throwing up his arms helplessly.

"Dear ladies, I am so sorry. I have just remembered an important meeting across town and I must not be late. Forgive me."

He goes to Luisa and kisses her hand. "Until later, dear one. Our toast has merely been postponed." He turns to Angela."Hasta luego, sweet Angela. I shall see you and your mother at the churchyard at four o'clock. Meanwhile, you need not bother with driving Senor Bernardi to the airport. I have volunteered to do so since my meeting is very close by."

"I've already agreed to drive him," Angela says. "It is no bother. I'll get the keys."

She starts off.

"No!" I say sharply.

She turns and looks at me quizzically. "I said, it's no bother." Then she shoots a look at Rivera. I take her hand in mine.

"You've already done too much for me," I say. "Better that you stay here safely with your mother." As I say the word 'safely' I squeeze her hand. Again she looks at Rivera. then back to me. She gets it.

"We've had so little time together," she says.

I force a smile. "I'll make it a point to come back as soon as I'm able."

I move to Luisa and say my goodbyes. Rivera listens intently to what I say and then we are outside in the car and driving away. I glance back through the rear window. Angela, unsmiling, has come out onto the front porch and is watching us go

For a long time we drive in silence. I am sweating profusely and not just from the heat. I am clutching the overnight bag tightly. Finally I say,"How long have you known about the blackmail?"

He shoots me a look and decides he risks nothing by telling me.

"From the beginning," he says.

"How did you find out?"

"Pedro told me." He laughs. "Yes, Senor, he is a policeman and yet he comes to me, his senior officer, and he asks me my advice. I have a chance to make a good deal of money, he tells me, not just now, but for months and years to come. He says the person who will pay is a very, very bad person and yet, because Pedro is basically an honest man, he is in a quandry. Luisa has just recovered from the auto accident. His medical bills are staggering and he has no savings. It is because I am also a friend of the family as well as his superior that he has come to me and I tell him without hesitation to take the money. I wondered at the time if he had also asked the advice of his father-in-law but I don't think he did. Cesar Montoya was a very moral man who believed implicitly in the law. He would not have approved."

"Did he tell you who this very, very bad person was?" I ask.

"He told me nothing. Only that he had something damning that was too valuable to ignore. That is all. But now Pedro is dead and I am trying with great difficulty to live on a pension. I think maybe it is my turn to enjoy this money."

"At Luisa's expense."

He smiles. "I have plans for Luisa. Believe me, Senor, she will want for nothing."

"Is this the same Luisa you were willing to pump bullets into only a few minutes ago?" I ask.

He glares at me and turns his attention back to the road. We are passing through the shanty town which is fast morphing into the commercial district. Although we are heading in the general direction of the airport, I am pretty sure I will never get there. As soon as I turn over the can of film I am a danger to him and he will have no qualms about killing me. How and where he plans to dispose of me I do not know but it could be at any moment, down some deserted alley, or an hour from now out in the countryside. If I'm going to get away from him, I'm going to have to do it quickly.

Traffic is beginning to slow as the streets become more and more congested with the Saturday crowds. Then I realize we have stopped a few yards from an intersection where a minor accident has occurred. A harried policeman is trying to sort things out as the two drivers rail at one another angrily. I see another policeman on foot coming from behind us to his aid. This is my chance and I reach over and start to press relentlessly on the Renault's car horn. Rivera tries to push me away but I won't give. The approaching policeman turns with a scowl and strides toward us. As he reaches the car, I open my door and bolt for the sidewalk. Rivera starts to call after me but by now the policeman is rapping angrily on his window.

Drenched with sweat, I knife my way through the throng of shoppers clogging the sidewalk. I see an alley ahead and duck into it. In front of me is another street and I run as fast as I can, picking my way through debris and swatting aside damp laundry that has been hung out to dry. I have no plan except to get as far away as possible. There is no refuge with the police. Rivera is too well connected. I am on my own in a strange city that speaks a strange language. I burst out of the alley and find myself in the middle of a farmer's market. Dozens of stalls with every variety of fruits and vegetables line both sides of the street. At a far corner I see an empty cab. If I could just get to the airport, I think. And then I realize that this is the first place Rivera will come looking for me. But where else can I go where I won't be found? Too late. The cab picks up a fare. I look for another. There is none. I cross the street, pushing my way past the shoppers mouthing apologies until I reach the cross street.

Suddenly I see him blocks away. The little car with Rivera at the wheel and he is cruising, looking for me. I duck down another alley and step into a darkened doorway. Despite the heat I am starting to shiver and I cannot stop. I don't dare show myself but I cannot hide forever. I glance toward the end of the alley as the Renault turns in, heading in my direction. I bolt from the safety of the doorway and run back toward the street. I am starting to gasp for air and a sudden pain stabs at my side. With every step it becomes excrutiating but I can't stop. I dash to my left out into the street and race toward a main thorough-fare with several large stores and office buildings. If I could duck into one of them and force Rivera out of his car I might have a chance.

I look back and the Renault is just emerging from the alley. He pauses and then he sees me and yanks the wheel to the left as he starts after me. I run toward the thoroughfare and am only yards away when suddenly the black Buick Roadmaster swoops by me and skids to a halt at curbside. The passenger door swings open and the driver calls out to me.

"Get in, Senor!" he shouts.

I look back at the fast approaching little Renault. I don't have to be told twice. I hop in the car and we squeal away from the curb leaving behind a patch of burned rubber on the asphalt roadway.

CHAPTER EIGHTEEN

With the skill of a Mauri Rose, the man at the wheel darts in and out of traffic, avoiding collisions by inches and sending pedestrians scurrying for cover like alley cats in a hailstorm. I clutch my travel bag and pray for the best. My chauffeur is grim faced as he concentrates, looking ahead for obstacles and in the rear view mirror for signs of the Renault. I do not know who this guy is but he beats hell out of the alternative.

Though I do not know the city I can feel he is edging to the west and as he does, the traffic begins to thin and he is able to pick up speed. His grip on the steering wheel starts to relax.

"My name is Sebastian," he says. He glances at me quickly and smiles, revealing a mouth full of gold fillings.

"Joe," I respond.

He nods. "I know. I am a good friend of Rodrigo. As are you, Senor."

Aha, one of El Jefe's boys.

I shake my head. "No, I wouldn't say that exactly."

"Oh, I think you are wrong. Rodrigo learns from one of his people at the big hotel that you are coming to Mexico City and he asks me to look out for you. Only for a friend would he ask such a thing."

I hadn't realized that I had suddenly become El Jefe's bosom buddy but in my present predicament I'm in no position to complain.

"I am grateful," I say.

"De nada", he says. "I am at your service, Senor. Where do you wish to go?"

"The airport," I tell him. "I have to get back to Tampico."

"That can be arranged," he says, "but I do not think it a good idea to go to the airport. By now Senor Rivera will have asked some of his friends to go there and detain you."

"Yes, you're right," I say, "but what's the alternative? It's a long drive."

"No driving, Senor. I have other ways."

He glances up into the rear view mirror and his face darkens. He mutters something in Spanish. I turn and look back. A good distance behind us I can see the little Renault and it has seen us and is closing the gap. Sebastian steps on the gas and the Buick leaps forward. There's a lot of horsepower under that hood, a lot more than the Renault can handle. But when I look back again, I see that the little car is staying with us. Sebastian notices it, too.

More muttering in Spanish. "I think maybe he has done some work on that engine," Sebastian says.

I look back and the Renault has not fallen away. I think maybe he is right about the engine job.

Sebastian reaches for the dashboard and picks up a handheld microphone from a built in radio. He flips a couple of switches and starts to speak urgently in Spanish. A voice comes back at him. For nearly a minute they jabber at each other and then Sebastian replaces the microphone.

"My cousin Alvaro," he tells me, as if that says it all.

"And what does cousin Alvaro say?" I ask.

"He says he will handle the problem."

Good. Just what I wanted to hear. I feel greatly relieved. Cousin Alvaro is on the job.

We are climbing into the western elevations now and the Buick easily handles the ascent. I look back. The Renault is still in sight.

"I know of a small airfield on the outskirts of the city," Sebastian says. "The police know nothing of its existence or if they do, they are wise enough to keep this knowledge to themselves. There we will find a small plane which I make use of in my business. We will use it to get you to Tampico."

"Bueno," I say. What I want to say (and don't) is, how small is this airplane and what kind of business is it used for? I can make a wild guess but keep silent. From what I can see, this guy is saving my life and it would be bad manners to raise even the slightest concern over either his game plan or his credentials.

After a while our road flattens out and we open up onto a flat terrain. We are passing through a farm area featuring rows upon rows of ripening corn or tomatoes. There are also areas which appear to be lying fallow but are actually potato farms. Small adobe homes are scattered here and there and white clad granjeros are working the fields. Some look up and wave at us with friendly smiles, probably because they recognize Sebastian's car.

I turn in my seat and look back. The Renault continues to dog us about a half mile back. I look over at the speedometer. We are cruising at 75 miles an hour. I know this car can go faster and I wonder why Sebastian doesn't put the pedal to the floor. Finally I ask him.

He shakes his head. "Oh, no, Senor, I could not do that. I do not wish to discourage him."

As I mull over his response, I see we are approaching a crossroads. Parked to the right and waiting to cross is a large tanker truck. Sebastian reaches over and turns on his headlights. Ahead of us the tanker truck follows suit. We speed by and I hear hear the growl of an engine as the truck starts up. I look at Sebastian. I look back. The Renault is closing but just as it is about to enter the intersection, the tanker truck roars forward and slams into the passenger side. The little car somersaults into the air and comes down on its roof, then rolls several times. I watch in horror as a spark ignites the gas and the car bursts into flames.

Sebastian watches impassively in the rear view mirror and shakes his head sadly. "He should have bought a bigger car," he says.

Again I look back. It is a horrific sight but I am grateful I am out of danger. I am also grateful that Luisa and Angela are rid of this man who would have brought nothing but misery into their lives.

We continue on for several miles and then Sebastian turns onto a dirt road that has been cut from the middle of a corn field. We drive on but slow down as we approach a wooden gate guarded by two men armed with tommy guns. Sebastian waves and the gate is swung open. The two men smile and wave back as we drive through and then take a quick right onto an even narrower deeply rutted dirt road. We jounce and sway and I hold tight to my door handle as my head hits the car roof several times. And then we are out in the clear.

Ahead is a large open sided building over which has been strung huge swaths of camouflage netting. Under the roof are two very small single engine planes, either Cessnas or more likely, pre-war J3 Piper Cubs. Three armed men salute in greeting as Sebastian pulls to a stop. We get out of the car. He points to me. I hear the word "amigo". The men nod and smile. I smile back.

A fourth man comes out of a small shack at the corner of the building and he and Sebastian embrace, laughing. Their Spanish is rapid fire and Sebastian seems to be relating the demise of the Renault because he waves his arms like a big explosion. More hysterical laughter. I guess knocking off former police officers is considered good sport around this crowd.

The fourth man signals to the others and together they start to pull one of the Pipers out into the open. Sebastian tells me to follow him and we go to the shack. Inside, it is hardly bigger than a kitchen pantry. There's a phone and a radio set up, a desk and chair and a built in set of shelves against one wall. Sebastian takes two wrapped bundles which look like loaves of bread and holding them up, tells me to open my overnight bag. Reluctantly I do so and he places the packages inside. A gift for El Jefe, he says. A belated birthday present. I am not at all sure about that but I am positive that I want no one with a badge poking around in my luggage.

Sebastian leads me to the plane which looks sturdy enough. I notice that an auxiliary gas tank has been welded in place just below the cockpit. I don't guess we'll be running out of fuel. Sebastian introduces me to the fourth man who is his cousin, Alvaro, and also my pilot who will fly me to Tampico. I smile at Alvaro. "It is very nice to meet you, cousin Alvaro," I say.

He smiles boadly. "Si," he says.

I look at Sebastian who says, "His English is only passable but he will get you there. There is no problem."

Alvaro climbs into the cockpit. I shake hands with Sebastian. I truly am grateful to him for saving my life and I tell him so. He brushes it off. It is nothing, he says, and should I ever return to Mexico City, he is at my service. I salute him and climb aboard the tiny plane, settling into the passenger seat directly behind Alvaro. He taxis out to the dirt strip and heads the nose of the plane into the wind. He revs the engine and then we start down the runway, moving laboriously at first and then picking up speed as the engine whines at high r.p.m.s. We lift, then settle, lift again, bounce up off the runway and then we are in the air and climbing. Around a thousand feet, Alvaro banks left and sets a north by northeast course for Tampico. I look left out my window and see the sun still hovering in the sky over the mountains. I check my watch. It reads 5:38. I try to remember the distance to Tampico. I think it's about 300 miles. I peer over Alvaro's shoulder. We're cruising at about 65 knots. If I recall correctly miles per hour is a slightly higher number so we may be looking at a four hour flight.

I tap Alvaro on the shoulder and I shout so that he can hear me.

"The trip to Tampico, it's about four hours?"

"Si," he says.

"Will it still be light when we land?" I ask.

"Si."

I'm relieved.

"So it won't be dark," I say.

"Si," he says.

I hesitate. "So if the sun is down it will be dark and if the sun is still up, it will be light," I say.

"Si."

"Does your mother-in-law sleep with you and your wife in the same bed?" I ask.

"Si," he smiles.

I decide it will be useless to ask any more questions and so I settle back and hope for the best. I wonder if there are any parachutes on board and conclude that this is a very silly question.

If I thought Rivera's Renault was small, the Piper is worse. I am jammed in with my knees up under my chin. I try to squirm to get comfortable. Even that is a chore. I crane to look down out of the window. That, too, proves futile without inviting major discomfort. I close my eyes, hoping to sleep but the more I hope, the more wide awake I become. I resign myself to the fact that my scenery for the next few hours will be a close-up view of the back of Alvaro's head.

But sleep does come, in fits and starts, and just about the time my left leg has fallen completely asleep and my lower back is screaming for morphine, Alvaro calls out, "Senor! Tampico!" It has been dark for the past thirty minutes, but as I contort myself for a look, I manage to see the glow of lights approaching from below. I am elated. My tortuous journey is about to end. Then I realize that Alvaro is bypassing the city.

I tap him forcefully on the shoulder and point. "Alvaro, the airport is over in that direction. There! See?"

He echoes me. "Si." But he doesn't change direction. Then I realize we are in a gradual descent. I peer but it is pitch dark and I can see nothing. The moon, so bright the night before, is now obscured by clouds. We swoop down lower and then I see them. Two parallel lines of dim orange flames, smudge pots, barely discernible from this altitude, but if Alvaro is concerned he shows no sign. He starts to sing what sounds like a Spanish version of 'Besame Mucho'. The plane engine mainly drowns him out but from the little I can hear he's no Andy Russell.

Suddenly the wheels touch down, jarring me and sending shards of pain throughout my body. Two more bounces and then we are rolling more or less smoothly to a stop. Alvaro flips open the cockpit door and turns to me with a grin.

"Bienvenudo a Tampico!" he says as he hops down to the ground. I squeeze myself out of my seat and hesitate in the doorway. El Jefe along with four of his underlings is there to greet me and I won't give him the satisfaction of seeing my incapacitation. I leap down from the plane and fall face first into the dirt.

Bienvenudo, my ass.

I struggle to my feet, my left leg useless, and as I do suddenly headlights appear as three cars scream upon the scene and skid to a stop. Armed men tumble from the cars and I recognize two of them as the hard asses who dragged me into the woods at gunpoint. Two of Santiago's deputies emerge from a second car and from the third, Santiago and Captain Iglesia step out onto the scene. Iglesia shouts something to El Jefe's men and they unbuckle their gun belts and let their weapons fall to the ground. El Jefe, who is unarmed, stands still, hands on hips with an amused smile on his face as Iglesia approaches him. Santiago hangs back as if to say, this is your show, Captain, I'll just watch.

Iglesia says something sharp to El Jefe who responds in kind. It goes back and forth. El Jefe laughs in his face. This does not sit well. Iglesia shouts something to his two subordinates who move quickly toward the plane as Santiago's men keep everyone covered. It's a full blown search but since it's a tiny plane, there isn't much to search and after tearing out paneling and slicing open seat covers, Iglesia's men alight from the plane and give a helpless shrug.

I look toward El Jefe's men and figure that one of them, or maybe someone not on the scene, is on Iglesia's payroll. How else could the police have arrived on the scene precisely when they did? I watch Iglesia, eyes narrowing in thought, and then shiver slightly as he turns and looks directly at me and the overnight bag I am clutching to my chest.

He walks toward me and puts out his hand.

"The bag, Senor," he says.

Well, I can't run and I can't fight and I'm too old to cry so I hand him the bag, trying to push a vision of a Mexican jail cell out of my mind.

He places the bag in the ground, squats down and unzips it.

He reaches in and takes out the two neatly wrapped "loaves of bread". He stands and holds them up to me.

"Yours, Senor?"

I look over at El Jefe. This is a man, along with his amigos, Sebastian and Alvaro, who saved my life. I may be many things but I am not an ingrate. I nod.

"Mine," I say.

He is surprised by that reply and he throws a quick look in El Jefe's direction. He looks back at me.

"And where did you get them?"

"A gift. From a friend in Mexico City."

"And what is this friend's name?" he asks.

"None of your business," I tell him with an abundance of bravado I really don't feel.

He nods slowly, then puts down one package and starts to unwrap the other. As the paper falls away he can see, as do I, that inside is a two-pound bag of coffee. He frowns, annoyed. He takes out a pen knife and slashes at the bag. Deep brown coffee beans cascade to the ground. He tosses away the empty bag and picks up the other package, slashing at it. More coffee. He glares at me, then turns and glares at El Jefe.

"Vamonos!" he says angrily as he stalks toward one of the cars. His men follow him. In a matter of moments they are driving away, kicking up gravel and dirt as they go.

Everyone stays very stlll. Finally Santiago speaks up.

"Senor Bernardi, I will give you a ride back to your hotel."

I nod and retrieve my bag. As I walk toward the Chief, El Jefe grabs my arm and says very quietly. "Gracias, Senor. You have los cujones grandes."

My Spanish is limited but I know what that means. I smile and then join Santiago. In a moment we are on way back to the hotel.

CHAPTER NINETEEN

We ride in silence for a minute or two and then Santiago says to me, "You are a most fortunate man, Senor Bernardi."

"No argument here," I say.

"When I learned that you had flown to Mexico City, I was curious as to why. I'm sure it was not for the coffee."

"No," I say. I like Santiago. I still think he is an honest law-man but I wonder how much I can safely tell him.

"I have known about this air strip for many months now. A plane flies in, stays but three of four minutes and flies out. There is no schedule and I have no informants. Even in daylight I cannot get here quickly enough to do anything. It disappoints me to see you involved with this man."

"Believe it or not, Chief, he has been very helpful in trying to discover who killed Pedro Castano," I say.

"You may believe that to be true," Santiago says, "but I know El Jefe. Even as he appears to help you, he has his own agenda."

I want to say, yes, he has his greedy sights on an autographed picture of Humphrey Bogart but I keep silent. We are moving through an inky black wooded area. The dirt road is narrow and Santiago drives slowly as the headlights do not reach far into the darkness.

"Did you believe you would find Senor Castano's killer in Mexico City?" Santiago asks, concentrating on the road ahead.

"No. Only a possible motive."

"And did you find it?"

"I don't know. Not for sure," I say.

"When you are sure, it would be helpful if you would share this information with me."

We break out of the woods onto a paved road and to the left I can see the lights of Tampico. We pick up speed and Santiago visibly begins to relax.

"I think, Senor," he says, "that you do not entirely respect me."

"I do, Chief," I say unconvincingly.

"But," he says, looking over at me. He smiles. "But can I trust this man who plays the toadie to a federale. What orders does he take? What is he afraid of? Do you possibly think something like this, Senor?"

I look away. He's pretty much nailed it.

"Well, I am not afraid, Senor Bernardi, and I do not take orders. But neither will I confront the man because he has the power to influence people who can have me removed from my job. So I do not provoke. I cooperate. But I tell you this, my friend, I hold my own counsel and when the time comes that the facts compel me to act, I will act, no matter what the pressure and no matter who I must go up against. Believe me on this."

He stares straight ahead, eyes on the road. I realize it has been extremely difficult for him to explain himself this way.

"Tonight or tomorrow I may have something solid. If I do, I will call you immediately," I say.

He nods.

"Bueno," he says.

Twenty minutes later we pull up to the front entrance of the hotel. Santiago reaches in his pocket for a business card and writes a number on the back. He hands it to me.

"My home or my office, any time, day or night", he says. I nod and take the card. He puts out his hand. "Buena suerte," he says as we shake. He's wished me good luck. I'm going to need it.

I trudge to the main entrance and step into the lobby. It's pretty deserted. Carlos Martinez and Burt Yarrow have their heads together over a couple of coffees and Martinez is making notes on a lined pad. I remember that tomorrow is supposed to be the last day of shooting in Tampico and they're undoubtedly coordinating travel arrangements and hotel accommodations in Durango.

At the front desk I hand the clerk my box of film and tell him to put it in the hotel safe. No problem, he tells me. He also tells me that my wife showed up yesterday and was very disappointed I had left town. Just my luck. Bunny wheedles a plane ticket out of Wilkerson and I'm in Mexico City playing Nick Carter, private detective. The clerk says she had to go back to L.A. this afternoon but left me a message. Probably my imagination but it feels hot to the touch. Bunny has a way with words. I'm not sure I want to read it.

Phil Drago emerges from the dining room and as soon as he sees me I can smell trouble. He corners me near the stairwell, annoyance dripping from every pore.

"Where the hell have you been?" he growls. This is not the same Phil Drago I last saw cowering next to the mimeograph machine.

"None of your business," I say. "Where's Henry?"

"He's gone on to Durango to check things out. I'm in charge now."

"God help us," I mutter.

"Look, Bernardi----"

"No, you look, dimwit. I'm in no mood for your bullshit. You made an ass of yourself the last time you tried to throw your weight around and if that didn't teach you anything, then you're dumber than I thought. For your information, I was out of town on business and Henry knew all about it."

"He never mentioned it to me," Phil says.

"Well, surprise, surprise," I say. "Do you have anything exceptionally interesting to tell me? If not, out of my way. I'm going to my room."

"Check out by noon tomorrow. We have two scenes to shoot in the morning and then a flight to Durango at three o'clock. Are you clear on that or should I send you a memo?"

"Got it," I say as I start up the stairs and Phil goes into the bar, probably to get lost in a Margarita.

When I get to my room I call the desk and ask to be connected to Ken Moody's room. The phone rings a dozen times before I resign myself to the fact that he's not in. I'll try later. Meanwhile I tear open Bunny's note. It is far from scathing. It seems she scored a dinner invitation from Bogie and Walter Huston and now has enough material for the column of a lifetime. She thanks me profusely for not being around to spoil her moment. And, oh, yes, at the bottom she professes great love and says she misses me. I'll bet.

I'm hungry so I clean up and head downstairs to grab a late night snack. It's almost eleven-thirty when I walk into the dining room and look around for Ken. I don't see him but I do see Hal Croves and Herrera in deep conversation, just finishing up dinner. I wonder if Croves will be following the company to Durango or whether he's had enough of John Huston. I guess we'll find out tomorrow.

I feel a tap on my shoulder and turn to find a smiling Phineas Ogilvy.

"We'd about given you up for dead, old top. Where have you been?"

"Thither and yon, my friend."

"Anything you can talk about?" he asks. "No, no, never mind. I got what I came for. Your friend is free, my paper is happy with my reports, and I have had the good fortune to best Mr.Bogart at chess, not once but three times. I shall dine on that story for at least a year."

"You're kidding," I say.

"I am not and with my work here complete I will be leaving at two o'clock tomorrow afternoon for L.A."

"I thought you wanted to be a real reporter, Phineas," I say.

"Oh, I do, old top," he says.

"Then I wouldn't be so quick to leave the company. You never know what might develop."

He brightens. "Ah, that sounds intriguing. But no, I really can't." He leans in and whispers confidentially. "I've been informed about accommodations in Durango. Simply primitive. I cannot see myself spending even one night in a no-star hotel. No, no, old top. Without me, I'm afraid." And with that he wanders off.

I check my watch and it's past eleven. The room has thinned out and I don't see a waitress. I may have to settle for olives and peanuts in the bar. Just then I spot Jimbo and Moe Levine at a table in the far corner. I walk over. They ask me to join them but I tell them I'm much more interested in finding Ken Moody.

"Not in his room?" Moe asks.

"Nope."

Jimbo and Moe share a look. "Maybe the cantina," Jimbo says.

"Kenny met this babe there night before last," Moe says. "You ask me, she's a high class hooker but it ain't my money."

"Ken's not real sharp when it comes to women," Jimbo says. "What's the problem?"

"I need some film developed."

"Urgent?" Jimbo asks.

"You bet," I say.

Jimbo gets up and tugs at Moe's sleeve. "Let's go find him," he says.

El Perico Verde is three short blocks from the hotel and we hoof it. We're still a block away when the we hear the music and by the time we get to the front door we are in serious need of ear plugs. The place is jammed. They are standing two deep at the bar and every table is occupied. The tiny dance floor is crammed with couples pretending they are dancing but there is room only to sway back and forth to the music. On a raised platform near the back of the room an eight man band plays with controlled abandon.

The first thing I see when we walk in is Bogie who is sitting at a nearby table with John Huston. Bogie seems to be nursing a beer and John seems to be tossing back shooters. Bogie sees us and with a broad grin, waves us over.

"Hiya, fellas," he says, "join the party."

"Like to, Mr. Bogart, but we're looking for Ken Moody," I say.

"The camera operator?" He looks around and points. "I think I saw him over there with some senorita in a purple dress draped over his arm."

"Thanks," I say and start off.

"Hey, Joe, hold up," Bogie says, getting to his feet. "You and I have got to talk."

I look at Jimbo who says, "Go ahead. Moe and I'll get him."

Bogie takes me by the arm and steers me toward the door. He looks back at Huston. "Johnny, order me another beer". Huston, slightly glassy-eyed, nods with a smile.

We get out on the porch and it's a welcome respite from the bedlam inside.

"Look, Joe, you gotta help me," Bogie says. "Under the best of circumstances, I'm not crazy about location shooting. I have this aversion to things that crawl and bite. Give me a sound stage and a dressing room anytime. The Paloma Blanca was okay but from what I hear, Durango's a hell hole."

I raise my hands helplessly. "Accommodations are out of my hands, Mr. Bogart," I say.

"I know that, Joe, but if I'm going to have to endure dust storms and tarantulas for a few weeks, I want company. Now this guy from the Times, Ogilvy, I'd sure like to have him along. He plays a mean game of chess and I'm going to need something to help pass the time. You see where I'm going with this, Joe?"

"I do."

"Good lad," he grins. "Whatever you can do. Promise him the moon. For me it's either chess or booze and I won't have to defend the chess to Betty."

"I'll do what I can," I say, deathly afraid that I'll be able to do nothing.

Bogie claps me on the shoulder and squeezes it. He heads back inside just as my two buddies emerge with Ken Moody between them. Ken seems to be an unwilling participant in the exodus. When he sees me, he cocks his head curiously, glowering.

I walk up to him and say, "How'd you like to help me solve a murder?"

The anger disappears and a broad grin crosses his face.

CHAPTER TWENTY

Ken isn't exactly loaded but he's feeling no pain so we pump him full of coffee. After twenty minutes he's less goofy and more focused and so I pick up the film negative from the hotel safe and the four of us walk next door. Ken has a key to the office building and we descend the stairs into the basement where 'The Cave' is located. A second key opens the door and we go in. Ken flips on the light.

The room's not big but it's well laid out. There are two Movieolas over by a work bench that supports a couple of splicing machines. Racks on the wall hold reels of developed film, carefully labeled . Some are unedited takes, others are partially assembled and all are identified by scene numbers and dates. Here is where film editor Owen Marks and his assistant work with John Huston, shaping the scenes from the various angles shot on the set. Nearby are racks from which hang strips of film of various lengths. These are tails and leaders from the takes being edited. They are labeled and saved until the film is actually finished and even then they may be saved for safety's sake.

At the rear of the room is a door and overhead is a red light bulb which identifies it as the darkroom. When the bulb is lit, no one enters or valuable film could be exposed to light and ruined.

Ken opens the box and takes out the reel of film negative. He says it looks to be about 450 feet which translates to about four and half minutes. He heads for the darkroom door, telling us it will take him about thirty minutes to run off a positive print.

Moe settles onto a sofa which is against the far wall. He stretches his legs out and folds his arms across his chest, closing his eyes. Some people can sleep anywhere, anytime. He may be one of them. Jimbo is pacing nervously. He has a lot riding on this film like maybe his freedom for the next thirty years. I'm nervous, too, but I try not to dwell on it. I walk over to the bench and look at the work that's already been done to put this picture together. The magic of the movies comes together in little rooms like this.

Tacked to the wall is the call sheet for tomorrow's shoot and I see it's a couple of scenes between Bogie and Bobby Blake. Blake plays a kid hustler who talks Bogie's character into buying a lottery ticket. I don't know Blake, never met him, but I remember Bogie telling me that he's a whiny little shit. I hope he tries his act with Huston. That'll be something to see.

Finally the rear door opens and Ken comes out, the reel of film in his hand. He has a huge grin on his face.

"I don't know where you got this, Joe, but it sure is interesting," he says as he threads it onto the Movieola. A Movieola is an editor's device with a six-square-inch screen for looking at scenes, marking where cuts should be made and synching up picture with sound. In our case we have no sound track.

We crowd around for a look as Ken starts up the machine.

Within seconds we know what we're looking at. Moe states the obvious. "Holy crap, it's a skin flick!"

It is indeed. We're looking at a bedroom set and this guy is laying back, arms behind his head wearing nothing but a pair of black socks while this babe is hovering over his groin, giving his dick a real workout. We can't see her face because her butt is facing us but then all of sudden she stops and she turns to face the camera and says something angrily. I can't lipread and I sure as hell can't lipread Spanish, but there is one thing I know. The raven hair, the heart shaped face and the bee-stung lips, they all spell out Violetta Munoz in the altogether.

After a moment a fat man with white hair comes into frame and shouts something at her. She shouts back. The fat man looks at the camera and waves for a cut but for some reason the operator keeps filming. I know something is wrong with Violetta but on the small screen and with no sound, I can't put my finger on it. Just then another man enters the frame. He comes from somewhere behind the camera and his back is to us. We cannot see his face. He, too, is shouting at Violetta and then suddenly she sways and falls off the bed onto the floor. The fat man and the second man kneel down beside her. The second man takes her hand and starts to slap it, shaking it, trying to revive her. And then the film runs out.

Moe, always the joker, says, "I liked the first part better."

Jimbo's not laughing. He looks at me anxiously. "What have we got, Joe?"

"I don't know," I say.

I ask Ken to run it through again. He does so. I'm still at a loss. Okay, it's Violetta Munoz in a porno movie but she's dead. Her father's dead. Where's the key to blackmail?

"I think we need to look at this on a bigger screen," I say.

"Only place I know is the Alameda," Ken says, "and we couldn't get near it before tomorrow." He checks his watch "We've got a six-thirty call and as soon as we wrap, we have to get packed for Durango."

"What about tonight? Now?" I ask him.

Ken shakes his head dubiously. "Gee, I don't know, Joe," he says. "The owner. Can you get in touch with him ?"

"I've got his card with his home number on it----"

"Call him. Tell him it's worth----" I take out my wallet and riffle through the bills."----fifty bucks American if he can open up for us in the next thirty minutes."

"I can try," he says reaching for the wall phone.

Fifty bucks proves to be more than enough incentive for Lin Po, the little Chinese owner-projectionist. He's waiting for us as we walk up to the front entrance. I hand him two twenties, a ten, and the film. He smiles with a little head bow and then opens the doors. He goes upstairs to the projection booth while the guys and I settle down into our seats. It's an old theater and pretty small with no more than 150 rickety uncomfortable seats but I hear it's crowded every evening. Mexicans, like Americans, love their movies.

The lights dim and the picture comes onto the screen. It's much clearer and easier to scan. I look for a clue, anything that will jump out at me and say blackmail. Four and a half minutes later I am still bewildered. I've told Lin Po to run it through at least three times so he is rethreading. What have I seen? Violetta Munoz doing the nasty and then screaming at a fat white haired man who I assume is the director. A second man whose face I cannot see enters the picture. More screaming and then Violetta collapses. What am I missing?

The film starts up again and my eyes dart everywhere on the screen looking for something that I might have missed. Then I see it. In the upper right hand corner. A mirror. A reflection. A man. And then the man moves and a second later the second man enters frame as before.

Suddenly the projector quits and the theater is thrown into darkness.

I call out to Lin Po but get no response. I get up from my seat and look up. The light is still on in the booth but the projector is shut down. I call out again, louder this time. Jimbo and I share a look. Something is wrong. Just then the light in the projection booth goes out and I see flickering orange shadows dancing on the booth wall. Fire!

The others see it, too, and we race to the back of the theater and up the narrow staircase that leads to the projection booth. The door is open and we dash in. Ken flips on the lights. Lin Po is lying on the floor, blood dripping from a nasty cut on his forehead. The film is missing from the projector. Ken goes to the wastepaper basket which is on fire and looks in. "Shit," he says as he kicks over the basket. The film is smouldering as it tumbles onto the floor. Quickly he removes his jacket and he starts to beat at the tiny flames until they have gone out.

I hear a door slam downstairs and race for the rear stairway with Jimbo right behind me. Moe stays behind to help Ken with what's left of the film. We open the rear door to the theater and break out into the open. The wind has come up and there is the smell of rain in the air. We look in every direction but there's no one in sight and we haven't a clue as to which way to run.

Back inside, Lin Po is sitting up and Moe is tending to his cut which looks worse than it is. He says he heard a sound behind him and as he turned he was hit and went down. He didn't see his attacker.

Meanwhile, Ken is carefully unreeling the film which has been badly scorched and warped. And yet, to my amazement, it hasn't been destroyed.

"I don't get it," I tell Ken. "In that fire, the film should have been ashes within five seconds."

He nods. "And it would have been if I'd printed on cellulose nitrate stock. It would have gone up like a roman candle on the Fourth of July." He holds up the film. "This stuff is cellulose triacetate. Safety film. It's brand new this year. The guy from the film company gave Owen a couple of thousand feet to fiddle with, just to see how it worked."

"Can it still be projected?" I ask.

"I don't know. Maybe," he says.

"Look, I don't know about you guys but I think I saw something up on the screen," I say and tell them about the man in the mirror and how he moved from the mirror and then into frame with his back to camera. They had missed the mirror reflection.

"Did you recognize him?" Jimbo asks.

I shake my head. "The image was small and it didn't last long."

"A lot of these frames can be saved," Ken says. "Shouldn't be a problem to blow up that section. Might be lousy quality."

"But we could get a face we can recognize," I say hopefully.

"Possible."

I take the film and hold it up to the light. The image is very small and I'm not sure about the focus. And now I am bothered by something else. We were obviously followed here by someone who knew what we were doing and who also knew we'd been busy in the darkroom.

I look at the others.

"The negative," I say in a panic.

With the wind freshening and a light drizzle falling about us, we tear outside and race the six blocks back to The Cave. The basement door which we had locked behind us has been smashed in. Ken and I hurry to the darkroom door which is wide open. Ken goes in and then turns to me, shaking his head.

"It's gone," he says.

My body sags. The fight is going out of me and I need sleep badly. I look at my watch. It's nearly three in the morning. I tell the others to go back to the hotel and try to sleep. They've got to be on the set and functional at six-thirty. Ken puts our damaged print into a film can and hands it to me and murmuring their apologies, they take off.

I sit down on the sofa and stare at the can. Now what, I ask myself. A round trip to Mexico City, a near death experience and I am no closer to finding Pedro Castano's killer than I was three days ago. Through the window a shard of lightning illuminates the room followed by a huge clap of thunder and I realize the drizzle has turned into a full blown storm. Just then the lights in the room go out as the power fails. It is pitch dark and I realize that whoever tried to destroy the print and stole the negative could still be lurking about.

I get to my feet and edge cautiously toward the door. Another bolt of lightning hits followed by an even louder clap of thunder. I peer into the stairwell and in that instant of light, see nothing. I move to the bottom of the stairs, listening for any sound that tells me I am not alone. Cautiously I ascend the staircase until I reach the main floor. I freeze in place. My imagination has me in a death grip. I tell myself I'm alone but I can't convince my body. I start to shiver. This is no good, I think. To hell with it. I make a dash to the front door, dart out into the rain and pummel headlong across the property, pummeled by the rain and whipped by the wind. I'm too afraid to look behind me. Miraculously, the hotel still has power. I push open the door and stumble inside. Except for the clerk behind the desk, the lobby is deserted. Dripping water all over the carpet I make my way to the staircase and start to climb.

As soon as I enter my room, I toss the film can onto the bed, cross over to the window and pull it shut. The nearby chair and a section of rug have been soaked by the rain but it could be worse. I click on the light and peel off my clothes, then slip into a terry cloth bathrobe I find hanging in the closet. I use a towel to dry off my shoes and then tear several pages from the phone directory, wad them up and stuff them into the shoes.

Exhausted I flop down on the bed. My body cries out for sleep but my mind won't cooperate. I look up at the ceiling fascinated by the patterns of light and dark that play there each time there is a nearby lightning strike. Question? Who knew about the film? Question. Who knew I had it and where I was keeping it? Question. Who would be in a position to know I was going to have the film developed at The Cave? Question. Who followed us, unobserved, to the Alameda movie house? Question, question, question and little in the way of answers.

I try to think back logically from the moment the little Piper Cub landed at the airstrip outside of the city. Jefe was there to greet me followed by the arrival of Santiago and Captain Iglesia. Iglesia reaches into my overnight bag and takes out the two packages of coffee. In that moment, could he have seen the box of film? Possibly. But that makes no sense. Iglesia was in Mexico City when Castano was killed. But what if he had told his undercover pal, Jose Herrera, about the box? Was it likely? Probably not. Possible? Most definitely.

And then another thought comes to me.

I get up from the bed and go to the small desk in the corner. I open the drawer and take out one of the photographs of the Castano memorial service that were given to me by Carlos Martinez. I flip it over. Rubberstamped on the reverse side is "Miguel Augustin- La Tienda de Fotografia- Tampico Hotel- El Recibidor Numero Ocho" and then there are two phone numbers. One is for the shop, the other for his home.

I look at my watch again. It's nearly four o'clock. I hesitate only momentarily. I have nothing to lose. Maybe for another fifty bucks I can get Miguel Augustin to open his shop way ahead of schedule.

I dial the number. After four rings, I hear a groggy voice.

"Hola," he says.

"Senor Augustin," I say.

"Si. Who is this?"

I hear a trace of annoyance.

"My name is Joe Bernardi. I'm with the movie company and I need a film developed right away."

"Eight o'clock. I open at eight o'clock," he growls, hanging up.

I think about calling back but there's no sense pissing him off. If he opens at eight, then eight it is.

I leave a call for seven-fifteen and flop down on the bed, closing my eyes and praying for sleep.

My prayers go unanswered.

CHAPTER TWENTY ONE

At seven minutes to eight, I enter the lobby of the Tampico Majestic Hotel. Although it is bustling with businessmen leaving to make early morning appointments and others checking out in time to catch an outgoing flight, a dignified hush hangs over the surroundings. The doors to the dining room where I earlier had confronted Captain Iglesia are wide open and I can see that, although it is busy with breakfast, there is no loud chatter, no clatter of dishes or clinking of silverware. The hotel comports itself with a sort of stately grandeur as opposed to the Paloma Blanca which is always in a state of disarray, noisy and disorganized.

I move down the wide hallway that branches off the lobby and is home to the upscale retail stores maintained for the convenience of the guests. I pass a European designer's shop for women's fashions. Across the way is a jewelry store whose display windows are crammed with diamond bracelets and necklaces. Next door is a Brooks Brothers outlet for men. This is a mecca for tourists, not peons.

Further down on the left hand side is number 8, Miguel Augustin's camera shop, and if I am not mistaken, it is Miguel himself who is in the process of opening for the day.

"Buenos dias," I say.

"Buenos dias," he replies swinging open the door and letting himself in. I follow him. He looks at me with mild amusement.

"You have film you wish developed, Senor?" he asks.

"I do."

"Then you must be the man who makes middle of the night phone calls."

"I must," I say. "Joe Bernardi. And you must be Miguel."

"At your service, Senor," he says as he goes behind the counter and flips several switches that turn on the lights.

I reach in my jacket pocket and take out a ten inch undamaged section of the film and hand it to him. "I need one of these frames enlarged," I say, "and I need it right away."

He holds the film up to the light. His eyes narrow and then he disdainfully hands it back. "I am sorry, Senor," he says, "I do not deal with this sort of thing."

I shake my head. "No, no, you don't understand." I tell him about the image of the man in the mirror. It is only this one section of a frame that I need blown up so I can identify who he is. Miguel is skeptical. I tell him I am working with Chief Santiago to solve a murder. He is even more skeptical. I ask to use his phone. A minute later I have Santiago on the other end of the line. I tell him where I am and what I'm up to. He is understandably confused because he knows nothing of the film and Violetta Munoz and the blackmail. I tell him he must trust me and he must also vouch for me with Miguel.

I hand Miguel the phone. He and Santiago converse in Spanish. I hear a lot of "si's" and "comprendos" and when Miguel hangs up, he puts out his hand for the film. Again he holds it up to the light.

"It is a very small image, Senor. This will not be easy."

"I understand."

"And the quality---" He shrugs. "I am not so sure. If I had the negative---"

"There is no negative," I tell him.

He nods thoughtfully. "I will have to make an enlargement and then perhaps I will have to make a second enlargement from the first."

"How long?" I ask.

"An hour. Maybe less if I am not interrupted."

I nod. "Do your best, Miguel. It is very important."

"Yes, the Chief tells me this."

He leads me to the door and opens it, flipping the hanging sign to read "Estamos Cerrados".

"Go for coffee," he says. "Come back in an hour."

Remembering Lin Po and the projection booth, I say, "I'll wait."

"As you wish," he says, closing the door, locking it, and pulling down the shade.

I take a seat while Miguel goes through an archway into the rear of the store. On a table next to my chair are a half dozen Spanish language magazines dealing with photography. I pick one up and look at the pictures. Birds, bears, mountains, deserts, wildlife. Then more birds, bears, mountains, deserts and wildlife. It is the longest hour of my life.

At ten minutes to nine, Miguel reappears. He is holding an 8 x 10 glossy which he hands to me. "It is the best I can do," he says.

I look at the enlargement of the mirror and the image of the man reflected in it. Miguel's best is more than adequate. The print is grainy but the man's features are instantly recognizable even though in this photo he is a good twelve years younger.

"Good work, Miguel. Gracias. How much do I owe you?" I say reaching for my wallet.

He shakes his head. "Nada, Senor. It is my pleasure to help." He takes the glossy and slips it into a manila envelope for me.

"This man in the mirror," he says. "He looks famiiar. I think I know him."

I smile. "Yes, you know him. Again, gracias, my friend."

I go to the door and with a little wave of goodbye, go out into the corridor. I start toward the lobby but as I do, a familiar figure steps out of a doorway and blocks my way.

"Buenos dias," Carlos Martinez says with a smile. His suit jacket is draped over his arm and as I look down at it, I can see the barrel of a pistol peering out, aimed directly at my midsection. "Perhaps you will be good enough to hand me that photograph," he says.

"Do I have a choice?"

"Sadly, no," Martinez says.

"Then perhaps I will give it to you."

I hand him the envelope.

"Gracias," he says.

"What now?" I ask. "Breakfast in the dining room?" I display a bravado I don't really feel.

"I think not," Martinez says. "Let us walk."

"Which way?"

"The elevators."

He waves the gun subtly. I start to move.

"You and I are reasonable men," Martinez says. "We need to talk in private."

"Whatever you say. It's your gun."

He almost laughs.

We get on the elevator and Martinez tells the operator to take us to the sixth floor. We ride in silence. The operator is a young kid and oblivious to Martinez' pistol. If I say anything I could get us both killed so I keep my mouth shut but I'm pretty sure I'm running out of options.

We get off at six and Martinez prods me down the corridor to the left. He tells me to stop when we reach a door marked "Escalera". He gestures for me to open it and as we enter, he points to the staircase going up to the roof.

"Are we going for the view? I've already seen it, thanks," I say.

He doesn't respond. I decide to climb.

At the top of the stairs is a door. I open it and we step out onto the roof at the rear of the hotel. The sun is up but it is not yet hot. A gentle breeze is coming off the water. Martinez gestures me forward to the hip-high ledge that girds the roof. I hesitate.

"Do not make this difficult for me," he says.

"I think the difficulty is all on my end," I reply.

He sighs. "Why couldn't you have minded your own business, Senor Bernardi? All of this would be unnecessary."

"I'm just naturally nosy, that's all," I say. "Maybe if you hadn't tried to frame Jimbo Ochoa, we wouldn't be having this conversation."

He shrugs. "I had to shine the blame on someone. With his temper and his well-known run-in with El Jefe's men, he was an easy choice."

"But not smart. It never would have stuck," I say.

"I knew that. I just needed a diversion to cloud the air. Once the company left for Durango, nothing more would be done." He waves the gun. "Over by the wall," he says.

I'm beginning to figure out his plan and I'm not crazy about it. I need time to dream up a miracle.

"Well, Carlos, when you told me that you used to be a film producer, I had no idea your taste level was so primitive."

"I did not make those movies by choice, Senor, but they brought in the money. My other films, the ones I was proud to put my name on, they were, how do you say it, artistic successes and financial failures."

I'm at the wall and I lean over and peer down to the cement courtyard below. This does not look like fun. I turn to face Martinez.

"I have to congratulate you on Violetta Munoz. Getting her to perform, that was quite a coup. I imagine she must have cost you a few pesos."

"She cost me nothing," Martinez says. "The woman was a degenerate. She asked only one thing of me, to make sure that her father got a copy of the film."

"Getting even with Daddy. Nothing new about that story," I say.

He nods. "An old story, indeed."

"And then in the middle of shooting, she up and dies on you. What was it? Drug overdose?"

"That is what the coroner said."

"But you couldn't have her found on your film set so you stashed her in some sleaze bag hotel where some sleaze bag manager would eventually find her."

Martinez smiles. "I enjoy hearing you tell me things I already know, Senor, but I think our conversation is now at an end."

Not for me, it isn't.

"So Detective Pedro Castano comes on the scene and starts sniffing around and somehow gets a hold of the film. He has two choices but being an enterprising guy with a crippled wife and a lot of bills, he opts for choice number two. Let me guess. If I have my dates right, that's just about the time the president appointed you to head up the Film Commission so when Castano made his demands, you went along. Am I close?"

"Close enough."

"And then maybe you arranged for him to get a part in a movie and then maybe another one and while they may not have paid a lot, he had a lot more coming out of your pocket. Every month? Every year? Just how did that work, Carlos?"

Martinez waves the pistol at me. "Step up on the ledge, Senor."

I ignore him. "And then when you show up in Tampico, there he is. The guy who's been bleeding you dry for the past twelve years and suddenly, you can't take it any more and you go off the deep end."

"No, Senor, I do not lose control of myself. This I never do. It is when he asks for more money, a great deal more money, money that I do not have, that I realize that I must act. One payment more, he tells me. Just one more. Two hundred thousand pesos and he will give me the negative. Senor, I am an important man but I am not rich. I tell him I cannot pay him this sum. He says he will have no choice. He will give copies to the newspapers and the negative to my Presidente. This I cannot allow to happen."

I look at him coldly, "All it would have cost you was a job. You committed no crime."

"My job and my good name, Senor," Martinez says.

"And for that you take a man's life. Just how good a name do you think you have?"

Martinez scowls at me and it's obvious his patience is at an end. "We are through talking. Step up onto the ledge."

"No," I say.

"I will shoot you if I must, Senor. Do not think otherwise."

I shake my head. "Sorry. Can't do it."

He steps toward me. The ineffectual little bureaucrat has

become an ice cold killing machine. "Do not try me. I do not bluff."

"I'm sure you don't," I say, "but you will have no trouble explaining away an accidental fall or a suicide but it'll get really messy if they find a slug or two in my body. Now if you've figured out how to deal with that, then fire away but you get no help from me."

Martinez takes a deep breath. "I am sorry, Senor. Truly sorry," he says. He raises the pistol. I think may have overplayed my hand.

"Senor Martinez!" a voice calls out. We both turn to look. El Jefe is circling toward us, a .45 automatic in a two-handed grip which he holds straight out in front of him, sighting down the barrel at Martinez's heart. "Put down the gun," he says.

Martinez hesitates. "Please, Jefe. A moment. I think that you and I can do business here."

El Jefe's eyes seem to light up.

"Oh? What kind of business, my friend?" he says, never wavering his aim.

"Ten thousand pesos," Martinez says.

"You have ten thousand pesos in your pocket?"

Martinez frowns. "No, Jefe, not in my pocket."

"Oh, that is too bad. I could use ten thousand pesos but I am very fussy about the people I will take an IOU from. Now put down the gun."

"I will make it twenty thousand," Martinez whines.

"How can you make it twenty when you do not even have ten? No, I do not think so," El Jefe says. "Besides, I do not like you pointing your gun at my friend. So now you will step away and put down the gun or I will shoot you like the dirty dog that you are."

Martinez looks at me. I can see it in his eyes. Sheer panic. He has a vision of hanging at the end of a rope and he can't deal with it. Suddenly he darts behind me and loops his arm around my neck, jabbing the pistol into my rib cage.

El Jefe moves closer. "Let him go." Martinez shakes his head wildly. "You have no place to go," Jefe tells him.

Martinez nods toward the courtyard below. "No, Senor, I have somewhere to go that is better than a hangman's rope and I will take your friend with me if you do not back away and throw your gun aside." To underline his resolve he drags me to the ledge. I sort of look down and then I definitely look away.

El Jefe stops moving. He seems undecided. I know what he's thinking. If he drops his gun, Martinez may easily shoot us both. He's debating whether he can get a clear shot.

"Jefe!"

A stern new voice rings out. El Jefe looks past us. Martinez turns, swinging me around. A grim faced Chief Santiago is standing about twenty feet away. He, too, has a pistol in his hand and it is leveled but I am not exactly sure who he is aiming at. Martinez, with me as his shield, is now centered between the two of them and his eyes dart back and forth, not knowing what to do.

"Jefe!" Santiago repeats himself. And then a curious smile appears on his face. "This man is disturbing the peace. Shall I shoot him, Jefe, or will you?"

Jefe's eyes narrow, puzzled, and then he, too, smiles.

"I would not deny you that pleasure, Chief Santiago. Please proceed." And with that El Jefe lowers his gun to his side.

"Gracias, amigo," Santiago says as he cocks the hammer of his revolver.

Martinez swings me around to face Santiago and as he does, El Jefe raises his pistol.

"I have him, Chief," El Jefe says.

Martinez's head whips toward El Jefe and suddenly he is shoving me to the rooftop. He screams, "Noooo!" and tosses his gun away, drops to his knees and covers up. He begins to cry like a baby.

I get to my feet as both Santiago and El Jefe approach. They both stare down at the whimpering Martinez. Then Santiago looks at El Jefe.

"I think your business is finished here. Hasta luego, Senor." he says.

El Jefe smiles and slips his pistol back into this belt. He looks at me. "Adios, amigo," he says. He nods to Santiago and then walks briskly toward the stairway door.

I lean down and pick up the manila envelope which has fallen to the ground. As I hand him the envelope, I say to Santiago that I have much to tell him.

CHAPTER TWENTY TWO

Santiago cuffs Martinez and we take him in the Chief's cruiser back to police headquarters. Even before Santiago tosses him into a cell he's screaming for a lawyer who I don't think he'll get to see for quite some time. Mexico is very unlike California which, for reasons I cannot fathom, is starting to worry more about the rights of criminals than the devastation of victims. It's amazing how brave Martinez suddenly became when he was sure no one was going to put a .38 slug between his eyes. I wonder how brave he'd been when he knifed an unarmed Pedro Castano to death.

I've filled Santiago in on the big picture, i.e. the corruption and the blackmail, and in broad strokes he understands what went down. For obvious reasons I don't mention the box full of cash. He says I'll have to stick around for one more day to talk to the city attorney. I don't mind. I'm not going on to Durango. No reason to. But I'd like to get back to the hotel so I can say goodbye to a few people I've befriended before they fly out. Santiago volunteers to drive me.

In the car, we chat easily. I begin to understand that his bluster over El Jefe is just that. Santiago is aware that, in his own odd way, El Jefe helps keep the peace as efficiently as one of those so-called "lawmen" from the wild west of the late 1800's, men like Wyatt Earp and Bat Masterson who yo-yo'ed back and forth between peacekeeping and petty graft from day to day and week to week but made sure that real crime, vicious evil crime, never took hold.

I ask him about Captain Iglesia who I did not see at head-quarters. Santiago shakes his head. It is very sad, he says. The Captain was called back to Mexico City early this morning. A very good friend of his, a retired Captain from the metropolitan police force, died tragically yesterday in an automobile accident outside the city. I look over at Santiago to see if he is jerking me around but, no, I'm positive he knows nothing about my run in with Pablo Rivera. The smell of irony hangs in the air.

We pull up to the hotel. I promise to be in his office at ten o'clock sharp the following morning to give my official state-ment. We shake hands and I feel as if I've made a real friend in this man. I suspect he feels the same way. At least I hope so.

As I start to leave the car, he tugs at my arm.

'Senor," he says, and then amends it. "Joe, this movie. I have read the script. It is very sad. Very depressing. And my people, they are depicted as greedy bandits. This is not the kind of story which should be told about the Mexican people."

"Not my department, Chief. Sorry," I say.

"You should be making a movie about the heroes of Mexico, the liberators, the fighters for freedom."

"Well, maybe so, but Juarez and Pancho Villa have been done to death."

"No, no, Joe, I mean a real hero of the revolution. I am talk-ing about Zapata."

"Who? Zapata?"

"Emiliano Zapata. I am his great-nephew twice removed.

Now there is a man whose story begs to be filmed. Mention this man to your Mr. Warner. He will be forever grateful," Santiago says, beaming.

I smile. "I'll do that, Chief. Thanks for the tip."

I get out of the car, give him one last salute and then walk up the front path, muttering to myself. Emiliano Zapata. The Chief is one pretty fine lawmen but when it comes the movies, he doesn't know dog meat.

It's just past twelve-thirty and members of the company have been drifting in since noon when the company wrapped. I go to the desk and check for messages. There is one and it's from Bogie.

> "Joe...sorry I missed you. Catching a private plane out at noon. Talked to Betty. She says she's start-ing to show so feel free to tell the world she's due in January. Parents ecstatic. Sex unknown. Boy or girl, either one will do. See you back at the sweatshop....
> Regards, Bogie.

I smile. He's definitely one of the good guys. I slip the memo into my pocket. Just then someone calls my name and I turn as John Huston approaches.

"I hear you're not coming with us," he says.

"L.A. calls, Mr. Huston," I say.

"Oh, come off that, Joe. It's John," he smiles. "We're going to miss you."

"I'd be pretty useless, John."

"Not as useless as that idiot author," he growls.

"Croves?"

"Croves, my ass. It's Traven. I know it and he knows I know it and he is one sorry pain in the butt."

"Well, I hear it's going to be a rough location. Maybe he'll quit and go home."

"Maybe I'll stick a tarantula under his covers and help him make up his mind." He laughs.

"By the way," I say, "I'm curious how you made out with Bobby Blake."

Huston glowers. "The little piss ant. He tried to help me direct his scene."

"I hope you didn't have to spank him," I say.

He shakes his head. "No. I just did forty-two takes of his close-up with no film in the camera." He laughs again and grabs my hand." Take care of yourself, Joe. Have a good trip back," he says and then he wanders off.

I start toward the staircase when I notice a single piece of luggage sitting by itself next to the concierge desk. The gold embossed initials near the handle read "P.O." I walk over casually. There's no one at the desk. The bellmen are all busy. I check the luggage tag. It reads "Phineas Ogilvy, c/o Los Angeles Times". I remember my promise to Bogie. Maybe there is a way I can keep it.

Across the way I see dozens of pieces of crew luggage waiting for transport to the plane that will fly to Durango. I look around surreptitiously and then pick up Phineas' suitcase and deposit it on top of the pile. Since it's lunch hour I'm pretty sure where I will find Phineas.

He is sitting alone at a table, feasting on a platter of beef and chicken tacos and drinking a local beer. He smiles in greeting as I approach and invites me to join him.

"Have a taco, old top," he says. "They are scrumptious."

I'm sure they are but I have other things on my mind.

"You know, Phineas, I never did congratulate you properly

for that amazing feat of yours. I mean, beating Bogart three times at chess. Unbelievable."

He smiles shyly. "I am a man of many talents, Joseph," he says.

"No, Phineas, I mean, unbelievable. Were there any witnesses to this miraculous accomplishment?"

He looks up at me, annoyed. "Witnesses? Why should I need witnesses? We played in the peace and quiet of his hotel room ."

"I see," I say thoughtfully.

"I see?" he snaps. "What do you mean, I see?"

"I just mean that Bogart is such a good player that no one will actually believe you did it, especially if Bogart denies it and I call you a liar."

"What?" he howls.

"How are you going to dine out on that story, Phineas? You'll be lucky to be invited for stale peanuts and warm beer."

"Oh, now look here, old top----"

"On the other hand, if you were to join Bogie on location in Durango and played him while people were watching----"

"This is extortion!" Phineas sputters.

"Absolutely. But look at it this way, you beat him three times, you can do it again. Unless, of course, your wins were dumb luck."

Phineas puffs himself up indignantly. "Sir, there is no such thing as luck in chess."

"Well, there you are," I smile. "No problem."

He glowers at me, his eyes sad and disillusioned like a puppy that's just been kicked in the butt. "I shall not soon forget this indignity, Joseph."

"Fine," I say. "Now do you have a notepad and a pencil on you?"

"I do," he says.

"Then get ready to write. I am giving this news break to all the reporters who still remain in Tampico."

He brightens. "Why, that would be me," he says. "And Alejandro Moreno, of course."

"Fuck him," I say. "Now, Phineas, here's how it went down."

He starts writing as I give him everything. My meeting with the widow, the letter left with the priest along with the safe deposit key, the discovery of the film, the attempt on my life, the attack at the theater, my brush with death at the hands of Carlos Martinez. He writes furiously and every once in a while, he looks up at me, eyes as round as Cadillac hubcaps.

When I finish he looks up, half in gratitude and half in disbelief. I assure him that everything I've told him is the gospel truth. I also tell him that I have given him this exclusive as a way of thanking him for going to Durango and keeping Bogie happy.

"You are a prince, old top," he says. "I am in your debt forever."

"Good. Now run, do not walk, to the nearest phone and call this in to your paper. Tell them you want the front page above the fold, a banner headline, byline in huge type and a substantial raise."

"Done!" he says putting out his hand. We shake warmly and then he hurries from the dining room leaving behind three cold tacos and a half finished bottle of beer. For once Phineas has his priorities straight.

I sit quietly for a moment, regrouping my thoughts. I, too, will need a phone to get the story to Bunny. God, I miss her. I wish I were on a plane right this moment winging my way back to Los Angeles and the warmth of her bed and body.

Finally, I get to my feet and start back to the lobby. On the way I spot Phil Drago. We make eye contact. He glares at me. I return the compliment. Jimbo calls to me and we embrace warmly. He thanks me again and again I tell him it's unnecessary. I'm going to miss him and Ken and Moe but sadly, it's the Hollywood way of life. Men and women gather to make a film and when it's over they disperse to the four winds. Friendships are transitory. Would that it were otherwise. It isn't.

As I start to climb the stairs to get to my room, Jose Herrera is coming down. As we start to pass one another, he puts his hand on my shoulder, stopping me. He smiles faintly. "Good work, my friend," he says. "Very good work." And then he continues on his way.

Once in my room, I call the switchboard and ask them to connect me to The Hollywood Reporter in Los Angeles. When I get through I ask for Bunny but they tell me she hasn't checked in yet. I'm not concerned. There's plenty of time to get the story into tomorrow's edition. I think about calling her at home but decide to wait. Right now I think I need a nap. Two hours worth of sleep in the last thirty-six hours just isn't going to cut it.

I turn down the bedspread just as there is a knock on my door. I go to answer it. Standing there, suitcase at her feet, wearing a gorgeous red suit and a cute little straw hat, is the object of my affections.

"Hiya, sailor," Bunny says, "wanna have a good time?" She flutters her eyelashes at me.

Without a word, I scoop her into my arms and plant a huge smackeroo on her lips, then drag her into the room along with her luggage.

"You're supposed to be in L.A." I say.

She shakes her head. "I got as far as Brownsville and changed my mind. Disappointed?"

"Hell, no," I say, kissing her again. And then I say, "Look, before things get out of hand, you've got to call your office. I have a great story for you."

She looks at me askance and then she takes off her little straw hat and slings it across the room. Her hair cascades down around her shoulders and she looks at me with an expression that would shame a fifty dollar hooker.

"Story? What story? I don't need no stinking story," she says and then she is back in my arms. Life is good.

THE END

AUTHOR'S NOTE

This is a work of fiction and most of the characters are inventions of the author. Others obviously are not. Dialogue in scenes between made up characters and real life persons like Humphrey Bogart, John and Walter Huston, Tim Holt and Henry Blanke has been totally invented but some of what occurred is based on fact. B. Traven, using the alias Hal Croves, did show up during filming at John Huston's invitation and his reputation as a revolutionary and an anarchist has been well documented. Ann Sheridan did visit the set and may have appeared on film as a walk-by though this is under dispute. Lauren Bacall was pregnant during the shooting of the film and gave birth the following January to their son, Stephen. As for Jack Warner he was unhappy with the film as it was being shot but reversed his opinion when he saw the finished product. "The Treasure of the Sierra Madre" was nominated for Best Picture and although it lost, Walter Huston was honored as Best Supporting Actor.

AVAILABLE NOW

The third in the "Hollywood Murder Mystery" series...

LOVE HAS NOTHING TO DO WITH IT

Joe Bernardi's ex-wife Lydia is in big, big trouble. On a Sunday evening around midnight she is seen running from the plush offices of her one-time lover, Tyler Banks. She disappears into the night leaving behind Banks' dead on the carpet with a bullet in his head. Convinced that she is innocent, Joe enlists the help of his pal, lawyer Ray Giordano, and bail bondsman Mick Clausen, to prove Lydia's innocence, even as his assignment to publicize Jimmy Cagney's comeback movie for Warner Brothers threatens to take up all of his time. Here's a short excerpt:

I get a coffee to go and head toward my office, stopping at the studio newsstand and picking up the morning Times. Lydia is still front page news. Once behind my desk I uncap my coffee and settle back to read the grim news. Somebody slipped the paper a copy of her mug shot and there it is, two columns wide and pug-ugly. Her hair is a mess, eyes hooded, mouth unsmiling. The lurid caption describes her as a 'femme fatale'. I want to call the paper and tell them they can have the photo or they can have the caption but they can't have both. I scan the article. The language is juicy, the metaphors borderline lewd. My name is mentioned. I'm a former lover, not a husband. I'm described as devastated and bewildered. Really? I had no idea. I'm quoted as saying I cherish the time we spent together. As usual when a story is sensational, facts make way for flights of fancy. In this case they are flat out lies. I dread the moment when Bunny reads this drivel. I want to choke this reporter to death with my bare hands.

The Assistant D.A. is also quoted. He says they are building a substantial case that points unequivocally to Lydia Grozny as the cold-blooded killer. I wonder how they are doing this without an eyewitness, a decent motive, or a murder weapon. Perhaps I expect too much.

"I can't believe you read that crap," a voice says.

I look up. A wiry little man, mostly bald with a bad comb-over, is standing in my open doorway. He has beady little eyes that tell you right away that he's trouble and his mirthless smile does nothing to contradict it. I think I know him but I'm not sure. He moves to my desk, jutting out his hand.

"Dominick Fiore," he says. "Herald-Examiner."

Now it clicks in. He's their ace crime reporter and his daily column features a photo taken at least fifteen years ago.

I ignore his outstretched hand and ask, "Did we have an appointment?"

"Didn't need one," he says. "I'm here to help."

"What kind of help?" I ask, his hand still laying out there ungrasped.

He finally pulls it back and uninvited sits in the chair across from me. "I'm going to tell your side of it, Joe. The heartbreak of betrayal. Your firm belief in her innocence. Your determination to see her exonerated. I've got it all right up here." He taps his head.

I nod. "Then actually interviewing me would be superfluous."

"Don't bust my chops, Joe. I already talked to her lawyer. He wouldn't give me the time of day."

I look at my watch. "Eight forty nine."

"Yeah. Funny. Thanks."

"Look, Mr. Fiore," I say, "this is a tough enough situation for me and for Lydia without you printing a lot of unsubstantiated trash."

"Not my plan at all," he says. "I want your side of it. The quotes will be accurate and I will deal only in facts. Come on, Joe, I know enough from talking to Giordano that you and Mick Clausen are going to do whatever it takes to get her off. That's good because you know the way the cops operate. They have the case wrapped up tight. Lydia's it. Any other possibility just confuses them."

I can't argue with that.

"Here's what I have in mind," he says. "You offer a reward. Information leading to, you know, that kind of thing. Somebody may come out of the woodwork. A witness, a new lead, a different direction. You never know."

I shake my head. "I haven't got that kind of money."

"Sure you do," he says. "Come on, you put up five hundred, Clausen does the same and the paper will kick in another thousand, okay? Two thousand bucks. That might get somebody's attention and if not, well, it keeps alive the idea that she's innocent and that you're fighting for her. So what do you say?"

I stare at him thoughtfully. He's right about one thing. It might help and it can't hurt. At the very least it'll stir things up and that's good. I get up from behind my desk and close my office door.

"Okay," I say. "What do you want to know?"

ABOUT THE AUTHOR

Peter S. Fischer is a former television writer-producer who currently lives with his wife Lucille in the Monterey Bay area of Central California. He is a co-creator of "Murder, She Wrote" for which he wrote over 40 scripts. Among his other credits are a dozen "Columbo" episodes and a season helming "Ellery Queen". He has also written and produced several TV mini-series and Movies of the Week. In 1985 he was awarded an Edgar by the Mystery Writers of America. "We Don't Need No Stinking Badges" is the second in a series of murder mysteries set in post WWII Hollywood and featuring publicist and would-be novelist, Joe Bernardi.

TO ORDER ADDITIONAL COPIES

If your local bookseller is out of stock, you may order additional copies of this book through The Grove Point Press, P.O. Box 873, Pacific Grove, California 93950. Enclose check or money order for $12.95. We pay shipping, handling and any taxes required. Order 3 or more copies and take a 10% discount. 8 or more, take 20%. You may also obtain copies via the internet through Amazon, Barnes & Noble and other sites which offer a paperback edition as well as electronic versions. All copies purchased directly from The Grove Point Press will be personally signed and dated by the author.